Armchair Hockey

Armchair Hockey

Mika Oehling

iUniverse, Inc.
Bloomington

Armchair Hockey

This is a work of fiction. All of the characters, names, incidents, organizations, and dialogue in this novel are either the products of the author's imagination or are used fictitiously.

iUniverse books may be ordered through booksellers or by contacting:

iUniverse
1663 Liberty Drive
Bloomington, IN 47403
www.iuniverse.com
1-800-Authors (1-800-288-4677)

Because of the dynamic nature of the Internet, any web addresses or links contained in this book may have changed since publication and may no longer be valid. The views expressed in this work are solely those of the author and do not necessarily reflect the views of the publisher, and the publisher hereby disclaims any responsibility for them.

Any people depicted in stock imagery provided by Thinkstock are models, and such images are being used for illustrative purposes only.
Certain stock imagery © Thinkstock.

ISBN: 978-1-4620-3292-1 (sc)
ISBN: 978-1-4620-3294-5 (hc)
ISBN: 978-1-4620-3293-8 (ebk)

Printed in the United States of America

iUniverse rev. date: 09/15/2011

Chapter 1—Out of Play

Hello and welcome everyone to another night over at Bell apartments, it's a windy night in the city and it's no less tumultuous inside where Gordie Howard, our star and main man of the night is having yet another fight with his girlfriend, Ashley, and let me tell you folks, she is not backing down anytime soon. No, my friends, there is no love lost between these two opponents, in fact, there has been a lot of bad blood between these two, and I'm guessing that part of it has to do with the wool suit in the laundry incident that transpired here last week. Gordie hasn't quite recovered from that last incident and his record's been sitting at 0 and 3 ever since and it looks like his chances at a comeback are rather slim, as it turns out that his big game plan this week of making dinner resulted in two days worth of flu-like symptoms.

Now, getting all set for tonight, Gordie's making some nice moves in the living room with the lighting of the various pillar candles, and here comes Ashley from the bedroom and presumably, she is going to be impressed by this romantic gesture and Gordie's looking pretty proud of himself as she walks in, but wait, what's this, she's up and running with the hands and tossing her head, it looks like she's really reaming into him for something, and yes, folks, it looks like there is an error here in our first round of play, it appears that Gordie has made the potential fatal error of forgetting that sandlewood and lavender can't be lit at the same time. That's right, sandlewood and lavender both have separate aromatherapy properties that Gordie has no doubt forgotten about and mixing it up could create negative or conflicting energies within their household.

And speaking of conflicting, Gordie is trying to defend himself with the best effort argument and he'll be backing it up with the "how do you expect me to know because I'm a guy after all" argument, nice double move there, smart on his part, but what's this? His best arguments are about to be deflected by the classic but always effective "you use that argument all of the time" and then the "I'm tired of all your—bleep out word here—and maybe if you could get your—bleep out word here—together, we would be getting married." Ouch, that hurts! Not the married card again, this is foul play, hitting right below the belt right even before getting into the thick of things-

We should get a call on this foul move in few minutes, but for now, let's take a short break to thank one of our main sponsors, as Gordie heads into the kitchen to grab a beer, a tall, cold Molson Canadian, Molson Canadian, the true taste of the game.

And now we're back, Gordie's got his beer and is pacing around the living room trying to figure out which one of the pillar candles to blow out but he can't remember anymore which one does what and taking into consideration the fact that each of these candles is worth about $60 bucks each, he doesn't want to risk making a major mistake by blowing them both out, so he's got to weigh his percentages. Now, in the past, Gordie's had a bad blow out percentage and the stats do not look good for him, in fact, based on the previous 9 times out, he's actually been wrong about 87.5% of the time and he can't afford to make another mistake here this time around folks, so let's see what he does here. Ashley's on the sidelines and she's looking impatient and is probably deciding right now if she's going to make the "you drink too much beer" comment, but knowing that she's already got most of the points working for her tonight, well, there just might not be a need to pull out the big guns right now.

Gordie does a quick about-face and he is back on the offensive, using the "candles don't matter, you matter" argument, and he is even going to throw in the L word for good measure, and folks, you can never underestimate the good and strategic use of the L word in these face offs, really, they can make the difference between wins and losses, but it looks like this is too little too late, as Ashley takes up the defensive line and she squeezes him in with the "if you really loved me, you would make me your wife," ouch!

The M word followed by the W word, that's two counts of foul play tonight, and she's cross checking him on the line with the "commitment phobia" argument, accusing him of being prone to this psychological condition that is debatable about whether or not this actually exists, and now, she's going to finish him off with the "I deserve better" argument, and folks, there is no comeback play for this one, there is no neutral zone for the "I deserve better" argument. This is a classic dilemma to shove your opponent right into a corner where they can't get out. The thing about the "I deserve better" argument is this: if you agree, you're finished. If you don't agree, you're classified as big jerk forever and you're finished. Either way, you're finished.

You're finished, Gordie, let it go. But no, folks, watch him go, he's following Ashley right into the bedroom as she packs her bags, that's right, the closets are being opened and clothes are flying all over the place! The drawers are being opened next, and he's still circling around her as she folds everything in four pieces and stuffs it into an oversized Samsonite. Which brings us to another moment from our sponsor, Samsonite, luggage for those on the go, especially girlfriends moving out in the middle of the night.

Now, ladies and gentlemen, we are being treated to a sloppy defense here as Gordie continues circling around Ashley and she is just deflecting him at every turn. There he goes with the attempt to get his arm around her waist, and she is going to bat him down with an elbow to the lower stomach area, ow!, that is one way to go, but no, he won't stop, he's coming back on the left hand side and he's going to try for the conciliatory kiss, but she's going to swerve her head in the opposite direction and leave him kissing air! Smooth move on Ashley's part, she has really dominated this game, and you should see how she makes this look easy. Gordie's flustered and he's still talking and we don't even know if he knows what he's talking about, but no doubt about it folks, it's stuff that we've all heard before!

And now she's making a straight beeline for the door. The bag is packed, the makeup's cleared off the bathroom counter and the picture of their last trip to Disney World has been knocked right out of its frame! Gordie's still chasing her down the line as she makes her way, but you should see the determination in her eyes as she drives for the door, she is going to make it, just you try and stop her and he's reaching, he's really reaching, making that one last L word attempt, and her hand's poised on the door knob and she is going for it, and now she turns to look at him and she's going to stick him one more time with the "you don't deserve me" line and it is done! That's all she wrote! Stick a fork in this relationship, it is done! The door slams shut, and Gordie's been defeated once and for all. What a poor showing, too, on behalf of the young man, he resorts to old tricks that might have worked in months 1 and 6, but have lost their effectiveness in months 8 through to 12. These mistakes will come back to haunt him and it is over. Will he recover? Only time will tell.

Chapter 2—Back to Single life

Alright, so there are pros and cons to single life. Everyone knows this. There are days that make you feel better than others, and then there are those shit days where you feel like the last known idiot on earth and wonder if you're ever going to get it together in time to prevent yourself from becoming that crazy uncle twice removed on your mother's side of the family who whittles old hickory sticks and grabs waitresses asses in every greasy spoon diner across the country. When I'm having my good days, this is what I have to say about single life:

Pros:

Beer
Hockey
HD
Hockey in HD
Pizza
Poker nights
Clothing optional days (mostly weekends, mostly pants)
Dirty magazines that you don't have to hide
No more girl shows about guys with names like Thad or sad girl music about crickets and love songs
No more fat free crap in the fridge
No pink
And then there are those days that I feel like a loser and here's what I think on those days:

Cons:

Laundry-
I usually don't notice this until I've run out of underwear and by then it's usually too late and then that's when I realize my girlfriend's been gone a week and underwear really doesn't clean itself

Dinner-
this is really not the worst of my problems, all things considered, but sometimes I come home to find out that I'm out of pickles and there's half a jar of mustard lying in the fridge and what I thought was food turned out to be my ex-girlfriend's forgotten eye makeup that I tried to put on toast with rather disastrous results

Bed-
Well, let's just skip over this one, I think it's pretty obvious what I miss in bed.

Conversations with my mother-
"When are you going to settle down?"

"Don't tell me that Ashley left you again! For God's sake, what are you thinking???"

"Don't you want to have kids one day?"

"Maybe if you put down that remote and stopped watching SportsCentre while she's trying to talk to you about life and other important issues, you wouldn't have this problem!"

And on my end of the line—silence.

I guess it's really not so bad, though. The guys at my office have really helped me through on this one. There are those guys that make me pretty damn happy to be single. You know the type that I'm talking about. Those middle-aged pot-bellied guys with the soft layer of fat around their necks from having so many home-cooked dinners with their wife and kids, doing home renovations every weekend in order to get away from their nagging wife who always yell at them from the kitchen and can't wipe their own ass without permission. Those guys always have the starched shirts with the collars that make them look like a 70s flashback of the bad kind. I feel for those guys, I really do.

Then there are those single guys in the office that make you look as boring as your grandmother. You know these kinds of guys too. There's Adventure Tim, the one that does everything to the extreme, the one that goes hiking in the Himalayas during his winter break and snowboarding while jumping out of helicopters down the black Diamond trails that make most grown men quiver in their boots. The kind that use kung fu moves in order to spray on deodorant. Everything is about doing everything to the max.

Then there's Don Juan Paul, the great mattress surfer of the West. Close-shaven like one of those hairless dogs, three buttons open on his shirt, status symbols of all kinds, wearing the Rolex that costs more than your house and car combined with not a hair out of place on top of his head. Women just fall like dominoes in the presence of these sonsofabitches. The guy's answering booty calls around the clock and he swaggers in every morning like his cock's grown another six inches.

And last but not least, a shout out to all the basement video game freaks that have their mothers bring them peanut butter sandwiches while they conquer the Universe as a half beast, half man in tiny metallic underwear with a sword the size of a Greek column. These are the single guys that I don't want to be and am actually glad that I'm not. They are the bottom feeder single guys that play naked Lara Croft in order to get a sense of what naked women actually look like.

So what kind of single guy am I? I am boring Joe single guy, the one that lives for watching sports on TV on my big LCD flat screen in HD. Not really tall, not really wide, brown hair, brown eyes—unremarkable. I might be the kind that would make his way onto every cop line, since half the population pretty much looks like me. Or I look like it. Something like that.

I am the beer-swilling, hooting and hollering freaked out sports fan who actually salivates when the siren goes off for puck drop the way Pavlovian dogs salivate for their dinners. I like to pump my fist after goals that I could never possibly score and I know my players stats better than I know the names of my ex-girlfriends. And the more hockey I watch, the longer that list gets.

This is the way that my week rolls out:

Monday—Fantasy hockey pool at Stan's place. Stan has a decent bachelor pad with three beaten down couches that you can't get off of once you're on and a coffee table with knife marks in it from so many dinners eaten off it. He also has three bar fridges loaded with beer, each placed around the coffee table so that nobody has to get up for one. Stan's the man.

Tuesday—Game night. We rotate between houses for this one so that our married loser friends can come out without their wives making a big fuss about what time they roll in. They never make it to the post game show.

Wednesday—hypothetically, this would be date night if I had a girlfriend. For now, it's catch up on stats night and time to bet on Pro-Line.

Thursday—Game night at the pubs. It's later in the week, so the marrieds are on a longer leash than they are the rest of the week and we throw in dinner at the pubs to give their wives a break from cooking. Everyone rolls home in separate cabs.

Friday—Poker nights at Dan's. We play with pocket change so nobody's out more than 5 bucks by the end of the night. We're a bunch of cheapskates and we all hate to lose, so it works out just fine.

Saturday—Hockey Night in Canada (insert music here).

Sunday—Errands, hangovers, awkward family dinners with my parents and my two married siblings. Everyone else looks perfect and glowing, kids are shouting and pooping in diapers and I'm trying to hold back from the urge to vomit both from images of domestic bliss and reminders of how many drafts I had the night before. Then I usually go home and fight with the laundry machine until clean underwear comes out.

So that's pretty much my single life. And I guess it's going to be like it or lump it.

Chapter 3—My Ride

My ride is so not cool but I like to pretend it is. I like to imagine that I'm off-roading when I'm in the middle of the city, muscling my way through lanes and swerving between wild animals like giraffes and elephants and lions. I like to imagine that my car's a yellow Lamborghini whenever I see carloads full of girls or girls sashaying down the sidewalk, looking light and angel-like in thin sundresses. And when I'm going down a lone dirt country road, with miles ahead of me and not a car or a person in sight, I like to imagine that my car's a tank, barreling down the French countryside, looking for enemies along the line, saluting stupid cows that are witness to my awesome power.

Okay, time to be honest. My car is a black Honda Civic. It's a safe, reliable sort of car that didn't cost an arm and a leg and I bought it five years ago when I just started my job. I needed something that was fairly good and dependable, although dependable is not really sexy or cool, so my ride really does all that it's supposed to do, and that's to get me from A to B.

I keep it shiny and clean for the most part, at least on the outside, so that people don't think I'm a total washed-out slob. The inside, well, that's another story. There's always room for beer in the back and in the trunk and that's what really matters. When I need to clean out the inside, like, when I'm taking a girl home on a date or something, well, then it's spic and span, but otherwise, it's like my place.

Chapter 4—My Place

Alright, I'd like to be able to tell you that I have one of those classy ultramodern chic bachelor pads decorated by two gay guys with a tv show, but the truth of the matter is, I don't. I actually live on the 4th floor of an apartment complex in one of the less fashionable downtown districts that's still pretty close to work, which is really nice, but not a fancy postal code in a high-rise condo with lots of windows.

I have one big kitchen/ living room, a bathroom and a bedroom and everything is fairly plain. The walls are white, you can call that lack of imagination, cheapness or just plain I don't give a damn. All of my furniture came from Ikea and was chosen by Miranda. I lived a couple of months with another girl for about 4 months once and all she left behind was some lacy underwear that's probably stuck behind the water heater, but in general, most of my exes don't leave much behind.

My apartment hasn't changed much since the day that I first moved in with Miranda, and she was all gung ho about choosing the furniture because it was exciting and we were moving in and we were crazy about each other at the time. I didn't care what she brought home, as long as it didn't break the bank and wasn't a pink poofball of some sort. She did buy a painting of a little café that she hung on the living room wall and it was the only piece of art that's ever been in my place.

When Ashley left, all I had to do was throw out the pillar candles that caused a lot of the trouble in the first place. I never got candles. I never understood why it was romantic to sit back and fill the room with potential fire hazards and then surround ourselves with them. I always look at them from the corner of my eye, wondering whether or not I'm going to knock one over with my elbow or maybe throw a piece of underwear on it in a fit of passion only to open my eyes and find out that I've set the damn drapes alight and realizing that about 40 local volunteer firemen are about to be invited to my late night rendez-vous and I'm going to have a lot of explaining to do.

I don't own anything expensive and this is not because I'm cheap. This is because I'm clumsy. I've been told this by many people. All of my exes who have lived with me remember me breaking something, never intentionally, but always smashingly. Because I never go halfway when I break something, I have to smash it to smithereens. Glasses, hand-painted mugs, teapots with handles that look like things, figurines of dancing women from the 19th century, flowerpots, clay pots, ornamental salt shakers (never the pepper, I wonder if that means something), everything that is marked fragile and holds some sort of distant memory for the girls who refused to speak to me for days afterwards.

Then there's the armchair. It's a lazy boy that I picked up on sale. I liked the fact that it was a man's chair. No fancy black leather, no cream-coloured sofa, just a good old fashioned brown cloth armchair where you could put your feet up and recline as far back as your back would let you. The kind that you take naps in. The kind your father would sit on in the living room while everyone else had the sofa or the floor. The kind that you only sat on if dad wasn't home and as a stupid kid, you would do your best dad impression, delivering a stern lecture on responsibility or complaining about taxes. The first time that I sat in that chair and had a beer while watching the game, I felt like a real adult.

The LCD flat screen and surround sound system were pretty much the only other things that I chose for my apartment and I'm pretty damn proud of it. You'd think that I sculpted the thing from my own hands, I'm so damn proud of it. But you should see how crisp and clear the picture is. When you watch the game, you can tell which players have shaved today. And when you flip through the channels and find that show with the women who live on that weird American street and who are always showing up at Awards shows and get a glimpse of Eva Longoria in all her primetime glory, you want to fall down on your knees and thank God.

Yeah, I love my LCD and surround sound. That's all my apartment really is, a place to store clothes, go to the bathroom, sleep and shelter my LCD and surround sound system. The fridge in the kitchen keeps the beer cold, but the stove's seen no action for years. I think it's an Electrolux because it's that weird yellow colour from the 70s and I'm actually afraid that if I turn it on that there will be an A-Bomb type mushroom cloud in my apartment, so it's probably better for everyone if I don't even try to cook on it. Yeah.

My place is relatively good. I clean it up when I have women over, but otherwise, it stays pretty much the same. It usually gets invaded by friends once a week and then the pizza boxes pile up and I'm usually tripping over empties to get to my front door, but it's all good. As a single guy, I wouldn't have it any other way.

Chapter 5—My Friends

I guess I have about five friends. I mean, I know a lot more people than that, and when I have my place invaded for hockey night, there's got to be more than twenty people in my place at any given time, but there are only five guys that I consistently hang out with, so I guess that gives them friends status. And not the Facebook kind. I actually see these people.

Business Dan is one of my oldest friends. Our mothers were friends, so we ended up being the default play-dates so that they could have coffee in the kitchen and talk for hours on end. He was always the kind that did everything well and kept everything in its place. Part of it was his dad's influence, since his dad had a germ phobia of sorts and he was always scared that the house was crawling with strange creatures with tentacles.

As a result, he kept his slick blonde hair perfectly parted in the centre and had perfect straight little white teeth and clear, sharp blue eyes. He's not very tall, but he wears expensive Italian leather shoes with heels on them and hasn't gained a pound since high school. He's the most metrosexual of my friends and we bug him about it every chance we get.

Eventually he went off to one of those fancy ivy league schools and he became all about business. He became one of those Bay street type guys with the Bluetooth and blackberries and always talking to someone at an unusually high level. I got used to him walking into restaurants and pubs yelling "Buy! Sell!" Everyone else looks at him like he's got a bad case of mange, but I'm so used to it, it would almost be weird for him to walk in and not do it.

Business Dan is worth so much that we don't bother betting with him on anything. That would be a sucker's bet. Business Dan's got so much money that anything that you would take from him would be chump change and he would just keep one-upping bets with you until you back out for fear of never being able to pay him back. As you can imagine, this means that he has relative success with the ladies, relative, of course, because despite the fact that he's an average looking guy with a lot of cash, he doesn't know how to deal with women. He shows up late, he forgets to call them for weeks at a time, and he sends them flowers with the wrong cards attached. He also gets the addresses mixed up and sometimes sends roses to exes that he forgot he broke up with via text message.

There are two classic women blunders that will forever remain in my mind and they are in a dead heat as to which one is worse: the breakup memo that he sent to one of his assistants that he slept with for a month and the time he got his mother day's lavender bouquet mixed up with his girlfriend's sexy red roses and thongs bouquet. His girlfriend was more upset than his mother, who just laughed and told him that he had no taste. His girlfriend couldn't believe he sent her lavender and called him a pansy. I'm not sure which one upset him more.

Stan the Man. He's a lot more fun than Business Dan. I met Stan at university and we had one of the messiest dorms in the house. Stan is the most laid-back man that I know and I guess that's why nobody ever has anything bad to say about Stan. Well, okay, maybe there are some people who get fed up with his nonchalant manner and the fact that he never gets pissed off, like ever, but how can you really get mad at that? You'd have to be a class A asshole for that.

Stan's fairly tall, really skinny and has a shock of dirty blonde hair that always looks messy, not matter what he does with it. Not that he cares. He has a perpetual smile on his face and always looks ready to party. His eyes are blue and full of mischief. It's fun to sit him next to Business Dan just to see the stark differences.

Stan will forever be a bachelor. He has the most hardcore bachelor pad with all the stuff that you could possibly ever want as a single guy within it, and he never, ever runs out of beer. He also never has girls over, probably because they would be too scared to cross the threshold of his sacred bachelor pad. We actually began to think that he was gay or something, but that really had nothing to do with nothing. All of his one-night stands took place elsewhere and there was never time for anything else because there was always something else happening (like another game).

Stan the Man is also the only guy that I know who has a running tab at the Beer Store. He always goes to the same one, which is about half a block away from his apartment building, and they have his credit card number on file so that he doesn't have to ever pull it out when he goes. They just tab it all up and send him an invoice at the end of the month. It's the sweetest deal and for some reason, Stan was the only one of us that was able to talk someone into it. Even Business Dan couldn't do that.

Then there are the two marrieds. We only see them twice a week and we don't bother inviting them too late on weeknights and they really bring the party down at bachelor nights at strip clubs, so we don't bother with that either. They're the lame-brained guys drinking club soda and wondering how late it is the minute that we get inside. Losers.

There's Georgie. Georgie used to be so cool. He was the third musketeer back when Stan and I were in university together. He was the grease monkey type that knew everything about cars and could fix anything in the house. While the rest of us reached for hammers anytime something went wrong with anything, Georgie was always there pulling out the right tools and telling us ladies to back off. The guy's as big as a bull from behind, huge shoulders and a tiny lower body that makes me think of old style wrestlers. He has brown hair, brown eyes and a constant 5 o'clock shadow, even after he shaves. And he can get us into any club because bouncers are afraid of him. Freaking Georgie.

Then he met stupid Paula and that was the end of Georgie. Don't get me wrong, when we first met Paula, she was hot. I mean, like really hot. Like the girls that you see in beer commercials type hot. The ones that have long flowing hair and tiny string bikinis and laugh while they throw beach balls around. That was Paula. We all understood why they got together and figured that things would be cool. But then we discovered that Paula was an insecure bitch. Okay, I don't want to be an ass, that's a bad word to toss around and I don't go around calling girls bitches, really, I'm not that kind of guy, but hell, Paula was a bitch.

Jealousy. She could not control her sense of jealousy. She thought that every woman who looked at Georgie was going to snatch him from under her nose. And insecure. Always wondering if she looks older than she used to, wondering if her ass is as high as it used to be and all that other stuff that pretty girls who are used to being pretty and not used to not being pretty worry about. Possessive too. Always calling him up at random times during the day, probably thinking that she's going to catch him having an afternoon quickie in a janitor's closet somewhere when the man is really crossing the street to pick up a bagel. Crazy bitch that Paula. Can't cook worth a damn and once she gets into the margarita mix during the summers, she's all over Georgie's guy friends like foil. It takes two other guys to pull her off, believe me, I know.

As a result, Georgie is always on the phone talking to Paula for one reason or another when he comes out with us. She even asks to talk to us to make sure that we're really there, like, where the hell else would we be on guy's night, right? But even though this happens every week, she still seems dead convinced that guy's night is a cover for some sort of bimbo that he sees on the side and we know that this hypothetical bimbo exists only in Paula's crazed little mind. The scary part of all this, though, is that she believes it so much.

Then there's Roger. Every man Roger, the most generic looking white guy known to man with nothing different or unique about him. Roger's life ended after his wedding day and man, that was one crazy freaking day. I still remember it now and swear that I can feel a hangover coming on just thinking about it. We got trashed at Roger's wedding, everyone did, even Roger. I guess that's where the mistake took place. Roger married this really rich country club girl that he met while he was traveling abroad, and her family was just loaded so they wanted to do the wedding right and have an open bar. Good for them sort of thing, you know, they felt that it was their duty to show everyone a good time. And man, what a time we had.

The unfortunate thing about this whole situation is that Roger also benefited from the open bar and took advantage of the situation as much as he would have if he was a guest. But he was not the guest, he was the groom. He spent his entire wedding night sick and slept through the morning after post-wedding brunch which was held at a golf and country club the next day. His poor wife had to go alone and she cried bitterly through the first half hour of it and then they missed their flight to Portugal, which was where they were supposed to go on their honeymoon.

His wife was so upset by his behavior and his lack of consideration on what was supposed to be the best day of her life, that she annulled the wedding the week after and moved out of town. Roger is still bewildered by this experience to this day and he still wears his wedding band and talks about his wife like she's still around. He knows he's an ass and that what he did was probably unforgivable, but he still acts like she's coming back any day now. He's kept their apartment the same and still has wedding photos hanging around. We've tried to tell him that annulled means over and that he's as single as any of us, but he insists that he was sober when he took his vows and therefore, they still count. So even though there is no wife calling up on guy's night, he's still rushing home early on those nights to see if she'll be there. Loser.

So those are my friends. Those are the guys that I meet up for poker and for game night. We're a bit of a crazy crew, but I don't know what I would do without them.

Chapter 6—My job

I wish this was a chapter that I could skip, but it would be pretty hard to get to know me if you didn't know what kind of dead end job that I actually worked. I work for the government. Yeah, I'm one of those overpaid public servants that everyone else in the country hates. The one that hangs out in my cubicle and eats lunch in a lunchroom with other public servants that talk about where they'll go on their summer vacations and how cute their kids are and why can't they get a better pension plan and other stuff. I hate it.

I make a decent pay and the work's not too challenging. My boss usually cruises by my office once a day or so to give me work, but in general, he lets me work independently on my various mundane assignments. I spend most of my time hiding out in my cubicle and hoping that nothing too urgent comes across my desk, and 9 times out of 10, it does not. It gives me plenty of time to keep updated on TSN so that I can keep up with my teams and to make my playoff predictions. Oh, and it keeps me from living on the street, so I guess I'm pretty grateful to it.

Chapter 7—My Wonder Years

It didn't used to be like this. This is pretty damn far from the life that I was hoping to have. When I was a kid, I was that dreamer stupid skinny kid that always dreamed of making it to the NHL. I played in the street with the kids from the neighbourhood and cursed every time that they made me play goal. I was a sucky goalie and hated wearing all that sweaty stupid padding. And it didn't matter if I was any good at goal because what I really wanted was the glory of scoring.

What I dreamed about was game 7 of the Stanley Cup final, playing for my Ottawa team in front of all of my friends and family, facing off against some brute Western opponent. Gliding across the ice, skipping the puck off my stick, swerving quick and swift past big hulky defensemen, charging the net and ringing it in off the back with a stunned goalie falling face first because he had never even seen it.

That was my dream. That was my only dream growing up. I spent hours after school in the middle of the street, living that dream in my head, playing it over and over again. Of course, it never actually happened. I wasn't even good at street ball. I'd usually get started in my zone and then Billy Breyer would knock my clock off as soon as I got three steps out with the ball on my stick. He was one of those nasty kids that came back from camp one year to stand a foot taller than half the kids in our grade. He was big and he knew he was big. He was good and he knew he was good. And he let me know that I wasn't.

Not that my parents were a big help. My parents were second generation Western European immigrants to Canada who believed in hard work and practical jobs. They didn't have time for this dreaming about NHL glory crap. They wanted me to focus on my school work and getting ahead so that I could get one of those great jobs, like lawyer or doctor, and marry a nice girl. That's all they ever wanted from me. It was their recipe for happiness and no other type of life made any sense to them. My father wouldn't put out the money for me to get hockey equipment and join a real team. My mother refused to wake up at 5am to take me to practice. They said that if I wanted to join a sport, I should take up soccer or running because they would teach me practical skills and they were cheap.

I was the youngest of three children and both my siblings played sports. Doug, the eldest son, and Liz, my sister, the middle child. Both of them could beat me up until I was twelve. But they played the cheap sports, basketball and soccer, where all you needed to do was buy shoes. They also were good enough to play on school teams, and there was no way that I would ever make a school team. Even then, hockey wasn't offered as a school sport. We didn't go to those kinds of schools. And there was only so much money and so much of my parents time to go around—so guess who got left behind?

I didn't give up. I was a tenacious, hopeful, stupid little bugger. I raked leaves for all of our neighbours so that I could buy my first pair of hockey skates. I thought about scoring amazing goals with every single stroke of a rake. I kept thinking about how incredible it would be to skate hard, the wind whipping cold in my face, hearing the blades cut through the ice surface beneath me. I would get so caught up in my dreams that I would sometimes slap shot the rake right into the leaf pile and like an idiot, would have to start all over again with the lawn. But it was all going to be worth it in the end. That's what I told myself.

By the time that I had made enough money for the skates, I couldn't wait to get out on the pond. Growing up in Ottawa, the pond was the Rideau Canal, 12 km of open rink space. It wasn't the ideal ice to train on. It was hard and spotted and had huge craters stuck in odd places where if you got your blade chipped in, you would go flying through the air. Not a problem, though. I still wanted to skate so badly that it didn't matter if the ice was smooth or not and I figured that skating rough ice would make me a better skater.

I was wrong.

The first few times that I actually felt ice was on my ass. Because that's pretty much where I was the whole time. I had these visions of gliding across the ice like a pro, but I really felt like a giraffe on rolling skates. My parents did their best to help me get my feet and bribed me with promises of beavertails and hot chocolate. The sugary treat was definitely encouraging. Eventually, we did crack the code over the years and I was skating to beat the band by my 12th birthday.

I don't remember at what point I actually learned to skate. It was one of those things that if I think about it now, it really seemed like one day, I couldn't skate and then the next day, I could. There were years of strained practice and sore asses and my parents saying odd encouraging things as I bumbled along with all the grace of a gorilla, but those days have all blurred together and if you asked me how to do it, I couldn't tell you. It just became as natural as walking.

Despite my victory on ice skates, my parents steadfastly refused to let me join a league. I asked them every year. I asked for hockey equipment every Christmas and was always disappointed by the sweaters and socks that came instead. What can I say, my parents were practical people. They didn't have money to drop in registration fees, equipment and endless road trips to tournaments in other towns. A skate on the Canal was harmless and it was free. And it came with hot chocolate at the end. So that was the best that I was going to get.

So I grew up skating in the winter and running in the summer. I could do both of those better than my siblings. I tried a few summers of soccer and almost fell asleep. There's something about running up and down a field which just bores the hell out of me. And I don't understand goalie for soccer. Why do they pick a person who's 6 feet tall to guard a net which is 17 feet by 14? How does that make any sense? I think that person is just basically there to distract the shooter into thinking there's a minute chance that they won't make it in.

My ball hockey days were pretty much numbered. My mother was always worried that someone was going to get their head cracked open on the pavement and tried to get me to wear a helmet which made all the other kids call me a retard. My father said that ball hockey was interfering with my studies and that it must be the reason why I was failing math. I thought math was the reason that I was failing math. Either way, I was going to get called retarded by someone, so I gave up and decided to be a good boy and knuckle down.

So begins the path of least resistance which characterizes most of my futile life.

I gave up the idea of playing hockey and instead became obsessed with it from the sidelines. I started to watch as many games as I could, usually going over to friends' houses because we had one TV in the house and it was in the living room and we were always watching documentaries to make us smarter. I spent a good part of my adolescent life in other people's basements watching hockey games. It was a great time.

Every one of my friends growing up had a finished basement with carpet and wood paneling and a well-worn armchair. Sometimes you could swing in them and we would make ourselves sick. It was always "dad's chair" and it was the one where he sat to watch the game every Saturday night. I wanted one of those chairs when I grew up. I knew that for sure.

I got a part time job at the local Canadian Tire and spent a lot of my time stocking hockey sticks for more fortunate kids who actually got to play. And when I got my paycheques, I would almost always grab hockey cards and books. No matter what my parents did, no matter what they said, no matter how hard they pushed me to become a lawyer, hockey was my life, my passion, my dream, my joy. There was just nothing else.

Then, when I was fifteen, I got my first serious girlfriend. Her name was Tasha. She was a beautiful girl with dark hair, pale skin and bright blue eyes. Her hair always smelled like strawberries. Don't ask me what she was doing with a fool like me. I was going through my gangly arms and legs phase and my parents had dictated a military style buzzcut for me during the reigning years of the hockey mullet. So I wasn't exactly popular or a prize. But she lived down the street from me and we used to see each other around a lot and I guess force of habit got her to thinking that it would ok to like me. She was also a couple of years younger than me and I guess there was something cool about having an 'older' guy.

Tasha was really cool and she thought that there was something cute about my loser obsession with a sport that I couldn't play. In any case, she'd sometimes sit back and let me talk hockey to her and show her all my hockey cards, explaining what the different stats meant and who were the best players in the NHL. We'd go out for ice cream and I'd take her to the school dance which was a good excuse to put my arm around her waist and I'd walk her home from school every day of the week because that's what boyfriends do.

Well, this lasted all of six months before she went away one summer and came back with tiny titties. She was one of the first girls of her class to actually get titties and we, the boys, were just starting to see them for real. Yeah, we all see them in magazines, but we never actually came face to face or within an arm's reach of them, so when it actually happened, we all froze like idiots with our mouths open, with no idea of what we should actually do.

Then the titties went to her head. She started thinking that she had 'outgrown' me or something and gave me this weird speech about how she liked me but didn't really like me. Something like that. I was crushed, as you can probably imagine. But I was doubly crushed when I found out that she had left me for no other than the big idiot Billy Breyer himself.

This silliness lasted throughout our entire high school career. Tasha and Billy became high school sweethearts of the sickening variety, always walking around the halls making googly eyes at each other and making out in the bleachers after school. And when Billy was drafted to the OHL to play with the Windsor Spitfires, he let her wear his damn sports jacket. And what did she do? Oh, she only became a cheerleader with long legs and a flirty ponytail who got straight As and went to all the right parties. And she got prettier every year.

Eventually, she accepted to go to the University of Windsor so that she could be closer to him and to cheer him on in his professional hockey career. The big idiot did go on to the NHL and was drafted 144th overall by the Boston Bruins. She became an interior decorator and they got married shortly after he played his first NHL game. I think that they divorced last year. He still plays with them. He's a big dumb brute of a player who skates badly. I take comfort in the fact that he only gets a few shifts per game, the big lunkhead.

As for me, the girls came and went into my life, mostly unremarkable, nice enough girls who were looking for a half decent guy with a car to go out with. I can't even remember their names or anything really distinctive about them. They were ok. I never went out of my way to go after one and the ones that made it into my life just seemed to show up one day out of the blue. I didn't work at keeping any of them around, hence, the pattern of relationships that I've managed to maintain to this day.

I did have one other serious relationship after Tasha. Her name was Miranda. I met her when I was in university. Like most people, I chose a university based on where I thought it would be cool to live, not where my best educational possibilities existed. I chose McGill because it was in Montreal and the Habs were there and it was where I wanted to party. Also, it wasn't far from home which meant that mom and dad could come down every once in a while with fresh laundry and some groceries. It was a total win-win.

Living away from home was a way for me to have all the things that I didn't have growing up. It was also the first time that I didn't have to share everything with my siblings. I had a tv in my room, so I could always watch what I wanted, which meant all the sports that

I could handle. I also had my own computer for the first time in my life and could be online for days. It felt pretty sweet.

I joined the ball hockey rec league with a bunch of the guys who lived in my rez and was at the pub every single night of the week, watching hockey and drinking beer. I got to know all the cheap sports bars in Montreal and which clubs the Habs frequented after games. Not that we ever got in, but it was still cool to know. I could stay up until all hours of the night and it didn't matter what I was studying as long as I passed, which was easy enough to do. I got my general arts degree, whatever that means.

Every Sunday I would grab a smoked meat sandwich and a pickle at Schwartz's. It was on one of these trips that I met Miranda. She was there with a group of her giggling girlfriends and I remember picking up her metro pass off the floor when it slipped out of her open purse at the cash. She had her hands full and her friends were less than helpful as they were already heading out the door without her and she was scrambling to pay and get out to join them when it fell.

When I handed it over to her, she recognized me from one the classes that we had together, a history class. I talked with her and walked her over to the metro to catch her friends and by the time she took off on the next car, I had her number in my hand. I'm still not sure how exactly it happened, I just remember leaving the station with a big smile on my face.

Miranda had long chestnut brown hair and matching eyes. She was incredibly petite and wore the smallest clothes that I had ever seen. Her shirts were the size of my hands. She had a great laugh and was a lot of fun to be around. Everyone who knew her said she was a really nice person with a zest for life. We always had a good time together and she gave me a lot of time and space to be with the guys and live my life. She was neat, organized, smart and had everything together.

Miranda and I were together throughout all of university. I thought that she was going to be the one for me and I guess by default, she thought the same. We spent so many years together and did all the obligatory couple things, meeting the family, spending holidays together, moving in together after we graduated. It just all seemed to fit naturally in the plan of life, that we were one day going to take the next step and get married, buy a house, have some kids. It just all seemed to be going according to plan.

We moved back to Ottawa together because it's a nice place to have a family. Our families were ecstatic. They kept asking me when I was going to pop the question. I kept asking myself the same question and couldn't figure out why I didn't have the answer. At first, I told them that I had to get a half decent job. I did that a year later, landing the desk job that I still have today. I said that maybe I would think about it after she got her first half decent job. She did so in that same year, landing a good position with the bank of Canada.

It was all coming together in a nice, neat, little package. You could string up a bow on it, it looked so wrapped up. But that's not what happened. I kept waiting. Waiting for what, I have no idea. Waiting for the right moment? Waiting for the romantic flash of lightning? I even tried to go ring shopping and pep talk myself into taking the big leap of faith. In the meantime, all of our friends were in the process of getting engaged and planning weddings and I was still sitting there, checking out the scores, asking myself stupid questions while she waited and stewed.

Finally, she got tired of waiting. She decided that we were going nowhere and she started seeing this other guy at the bank, this straight-laced, suit-wearing sedate monkey of a man who basically said yes to everything that came his way. Don't get me wrong, this isn't sour grapes here, but the guy is so harmless and ineffectual that it bores me to even shake his hand. But he was the kind of guy that she was looking for, reliable, nice, ready to settle down with a nice girl and start a little family. They both believed in the same happiness formula that my parents believed in, and I guess that's why things worked for them and not for us.

Since then, my love life has gone back to being a revolving door of unremarkable women. I don't know why. Maybe it's because I don't make good choices. Maybe it's because it seems like the women happen to me rather than me chasing them down like the manly hunter that I'm supposed to be. And maybe it's because I'm too busy watching sports on TV to give someone my heart and devotion and other stuff that you give your partner. And then there's the classic reason: I never met the one.

I'm not sure what I would have done differently with my life, but I can tell you one thing. If I had never met Miranda, I never would have accepted this boring ass dead end job. I'm not sure what I would have done instead. I guess there was any number of things that I could have done. If I had really been serious about a career in sports, I would have gone into that somehow. But how was I really to know? I never got a chance to be in sports because my parents discouraged it. I was never a serious student, so I didn't get into a really interesting field. Maybe I'm just not smart or remarkable and I'm really as mediocre as my job?

These are the thoughts that plague me during idle Tuesdays in the office. This is probably also the reason why I think so much about sports instead. They make more sense to me. When I spend long hours thinking about them and analyzing them, my conclusions also make sense to me. I astound myself with my hockey by the sidelines brilliance. Allow me to share it with you.

Chapter 8—Fanhood

There are three big things which determine your team loyalty in pro sports and they are the base of all fanhood.

1. Geography
Within a certain distance of a team, you will love it.
Within a certain town/region, you will love it.
If you love your town, you will love your team by extension.
Also, within a certain distance of Toronto, you will love the Leafs.
Within a certain distance away from Toronto, you will hate the Leafs.
The only team that is immune to this are the Habs: they are loved internationally.

2. Genealogy
Your father cheers for them, you cheer for them.
You're descended from them, you cheer for them.
Your family loyalty is your loyalty; so it doesn't matter at that point who they are or why they love them, you love them.

3. Events in history
Either your own or just in history itself, events in history mark you and they make you love/ hate certain things. It could be something as important as an iconic player or moment, or as mundane as an ugly jersey or terrible logo.
And then there are those hockey type historians who love the original six, just because they are the original six.

Then there's a third and strange, unofficial reason that sometimes happens to people and is linked to none of the above: love. Just love. With no rhyme nor reason.

Chapter 9—My teams

First up: My conference! East! East! East! Woo woo woo!

I love the Eastern Conference because it's all about speed. It's all slick, skill, puck handling and dodging around dummy defensemen like they're pylons. I love the tradition of the teams in the East like my Canadian favourites. And you have to love any Conference that has the Habs.

The Ottawa Senators

TIL DEATH! This is the team that has my loyalty branded into my system, this is the only thing that I'm happy to have my city's name attached to, not Parliament, not the Supreme Court, not the museums and other crap, it's the freaking SENATORS.

The Montreal Canadiens (Habs)

IF Ottawa fails, and that's a pretty big IF I'll tell you that, then the Habs are where it's at. They have a freaking legendary legion of fans that almost make hockey hooliganism a reality. Gotta love that team and gotta love those fans. My McGill years have instilled a love inside of me for the Habs that I could never shake. But if they're playing Ottawa, I hope that we crush their hopes and dreams.

The Toronto Maple Leafs

We're number 12! We're number 12! 1-2—twelve!

I hate the Leafs. It may be geography, it may be history, it may be because Toronto thinks it's the epicenter of the universe and that they're going to win the Cup every year, it may also be because they hate US so much, but I really, really, really hate the Leafs.

The Boston Bruins

Gotta respect the team that's being led out the gate by Chara. The man's a freaking Goliath.

The Buffalo Sabres

It's Miller Time! There is no good reason for this team to show up on opening day except for their world class goaltending. Unreal.

The Carolina Hurricanes

The what? Oh yeah, they have one of the Staal brothers, which is their big claim to fame after their strange miracle Cup Run and that was the weird year that nobody was paying attention.

The Atlanta Thrashers

The who?

The Pittsburgh Penguins

Sid the Kid! Malkin can't speak English but he knows how to kick your butt! That's all the English you gotta know.

New Jersey Devils

Freaking Jersey. Their game style is about as dynamic as a board meeting and they're in freaking Jersey.

Philadelphia Flyers

Get out of town, you bums!

Washington Capitals

Ovechkin. Gotta keep an eye on that guy. Cute girlfriend, too.

The New York Rangers

Isn't Avery dating that Elisha Cuthbert chick? Freaking hot. Oh yeah, and I hear they play hockey too.

The New York Islanders

How did New York get two teams anyway?

The Florida Panthers

They're okay. They have cheerleaders. Nice.

The Tampa Bay Lightning

Forget lightning striking twice, they should work on striking once.

On to the West (which will be won!):

The Detroit Red Wings

Tough to beat.

San Jose Sharks

That's a bitching logo.

Minnesota Wild

Tame.

Anaheim Ducks

Dirty ducks. Get away with murder. They suck.

Dallas Stars

Yawn.

Calgary Flames

Flaming.

Edmonton Oilers

The day that they traded Wayne was the day that they ceased to do anything right.

Vancouver Canucks

Should be a hell of lot better than they actually are, but hell, what are you gonna do?

Nashville Predators

Home of the country singers of tomorrow. Does anyone down there know what hockey is???

Colorado Avalanche

Bury 'em.

Chicago Blackhawks

Stick to basketball.

Phoenix Coyotes

How does a team coached by the Great One suck the big one like this???

Columbus Blue Jackets

Oh no! Here come the jackets! I'm so scared. What do we do when the pants show up?

St. Louis Blues

Memo to you, St. Louis—this is a music type, not a sports team.

Los Angeles Kings

Take out the Hoover—lots of sucking going on here.

Chapter 10—The start of the season

As far as I'm concerned, Ashley did me a favour by leaving right before the start of the season. No more candles and cuddling in front of freaking *Dancing with the Stars* while she tries to explain to me how hard dancing really is while some guy cha-chas with his butt out in skinny pants. No, hell no, now that she's gone, it's all hockey, all the time.

So it's the beginning of the 2006-2007 season and the Sens look pretty good. I have to admit that I have something of a man crush on Ottawa's main line of Spezza, Alfredsson and Heatley. That's because they're just so damn good together. They're like a holy trinity of goal scoring magic. Not that they're appreciated properly and that's partly because of the non-loyalty of the fans in this town.

There are so many people who jump on the Sens bandwagon when they're doing well, so many people dressed up in red and generally making asses of themselves and buying up merchandise like hot stocks. Then the crash comes around, they start slipping in one way or another, and the city drops them like hot rocks. Cynical bureaucrats on buses always snarl out of the sides of their mouths and call them a bunch of overpaid no-good bums, as if other people in this city don't think the same way about them. But it's pretty much a guarantee that a city full of six-figure bureaucrats is not going to be pleased with a group of under-performing millionnaires. Whatever. This town's made all wrong.

And then the news. The stupid news. The local news is always covering issues like potholes and parking meters, and then there's always a focus on the Sens and they send reporters in to ask them dumb questions. I don't get why they talk to players. I'm a sports fan, really, and I understand that there's strategy and other things involved with the game, and there's a lot of smart stuff going on and most of it's going on in the backroom and stuff, but damn it all to hell, why talk to the damn players?

First of all, if there's strategy and smart stuff to know, THEY ARE NOT GOING TO TELL YOU. That's their little team secret and they would be toast if the opposition got a hold of them, this is like freaking modern warfare, you don't send your game plans over to them. Second of all, THEY ARE NOT THE ONES TO ASK. The guys who have the goods are all of the ones who work behind the scenes and watch the game on 8 flat screens and freeze frame things in super slow motion to see where everyone is on the ice and where they should be. Third of all, THEY ARE NOT VERY INTERESTING. Some of them are uninteresting on purpose, giving you the script answers that are safe and meaningless, while others are smarter on the ice than they are in real life. They're all going to give you the same answers, which are, as follows:

"We're going to give it our best, give it 110%, play hard, play smart, that's our game plan."

Read: We must win game, we go win game. Duh.

"We're going to have to play hard to win, so that's what we're going to do."

Read: We must win game, we go win game. Duh.

"We didn't have our game on the other night, it wasn't our best time out, it wasn't our best effort, but you just have to forget it and put it behind you and move on."

Read: We really suck but we have to win game, so we go win game. Duh.

And this one is really great:

"We're going to take it day by day."

Read: I don't understand the question.

Not that you can lay all the blame on the players themselves. Think about the reporters and the dumb ass questions that they sometimes ask. They almost surpass the answers in their idiocy. Like this:

"Why do you think you're losing the game?"

Uh . . . because we don't put pucks in the net. How's that for an answer? Figure it out, Einstein, if the score's 5 to 0 and you're getting shut out by the other team, you're probably losing because nothing's going in. Duh . . . like, watch the game for three seconds, moron, you'll figure that out pretty fast.

"How do you think the injuries on your bench will affect your game performance?"

Uh . . . well, considering that some of the strongest, fastest, sharpest and greatest players might be out of the lineup, let's see . . . bad???

"How do you think the team will be affected by the return of one of its strongest, most talented players?"

Uh . . . well, considering that he's one of the strongest, most talented, let's see . . . . good???

"How has your team been affected recently by all the negative press that it's been receiving?"

Oh, well, just fine and dandy, media. Everyone likes to get poked fun at, everyone loves it when you're known as a group of overpaid no-good bums, I mean, isn't that the reason why people get involved in sports in the first place? Isn't that the reason why we train for hours on end and neglect our girlfriends, wives and children, so that people can call us a bunch of nasty names and let us know in a very public way that they think that we're about as good as the goop you find underneath bleachers at old arenas? Isn't that worth getting slammed into boards and risking concussions every time that we get checked by massive opponents, ramming us at 110 miles an hour? And better yet, isn't that great thanks for the hours of charity work and autographs that we sign for sick kids in hospitals?

I don't get this thing with the fans from one town to another. You get a town like Montreal where they're ready to turn over cars in the street if something happens with their team, they hoot and holler and pound on tables in every sports pub up and down the street and they'll even dance in the streets with their shirts off like a drunken Mardi Gras (is there any other kind?)

Then, you get a town like Toronto, where the die-hard fans paint themselves in blue and white and scream their lungs out every time something happens on the ice and they follow the Leafs news more closely than they follow the Afghanistan mission. These guys will pound their chests like gorillas in defense of their team, even if they're stuck at 12 and have been out of the playoffs for several years.

And then you get a town like Ottawa, the town of the frustrated bureaucrat, one of which, I am sorry to say, I am. Goddamn it, going to a game at Scotiabank Place is like sitting in the House of Commons, it's so damn quiet except for the odd guy yelling, who is usually one from the opposition. You get that group of lazy-eyed bureaucrats and lawyers, some of whom are there to woo clients and others who are there in the hope that their kids will leave them alone for a couple of hours if they sit them down in the seats and supply them with hot dog money. And there's always one row of frat guys, getting drunker and having more fun than half the people there, if only they could remember where they were.

Then, by the time that you get into the last few minutes of the third period, rows of people start to leave. Literally, rows of people start filing out in single file like they're late for recess. And that's because they want to get out of the parking lot a bit early so that they can go home and get to work the next day. The town that shuts down at 5pm. A highway full of minivans. What a following. And these are the same people that give them crap later on when they lose. Whatever.

Of course, the leaving early thing wouldn't happen if we had the smarts to build the arena downtown rather than out in Kookie Kutter Kanata where all the houses look the same. It's a good half hour away from downtown on the Queensway, depending on the time of day and the traffic flow, but either way, it's not exactly what you would call central.

To make matters worse, the traffic is always crazy during rush hour, and that's the exact time frame where people want to get to the game for the 7pm puck drop—so the traffic is literally jammed up for miles with fans competing with disheveled parents trying to get home to make dinner. By the time that you actually survive traffic without pummeling something on the way, you end up in this overgrown parking lot with only two entrances and you're stuck paying $11 to park your damn car.

So not only do you pay top dollar to go to the game, you have to fight close to an hour or so worth of traffic, jam your car between 6 other cars into a packed parking lot which is the same size as an adult high school, pay even more to park there, pay even more for food and beer, and then find your way to your seat. It's a wonder that anyone goes at all, considering that most of us are angry before we even enter the arena.

But you can't stop the hardcore sports fan, so close to 15,000 people do it every game night. It's something of a miracle on ice.

In any case, I don't care what anyone says, this is still my team and I'll still bet on them in my fantasy pool even if people call me a sucker, they've got a ton of talent on the bench and I think they're going to be just fine. The guys at my office beg to differ, on the other hand, and they're putting big bucks on the Habs and the Calgary Flames. I'd try and follow the Western Conference if I could, but I'd have to suffer insomnia for that to happen, since the games are always starting off at 10pm and I'm on the Eastern side of the country and as far as I'm concerned, Manitoba is out West.

Sometimes I can catch the double header on the weekends and it's great to watch them bang it up during Hockey Night in Canada, but by then, I've watched so much hockey that everything in the room starts to look like pucks and I know then that it's time to do something else. Hockey blind. It happens every once in awhile.

Chapter 11—Freaking Monday

Freaking Monday. Going back to the office the first day of the week is always somewhat painful, especially since Sunday dinner is always the same. Getting together with the family and having my siblings kids jump all over me like I was one of those rubber inflatable house things and my mom telling me that she's heard about some single girl who's a friend of someone else's friend and has a great personality. I hate hearing this story and I hear it so many times.

I actually made the mistake of going on one of these setups, and it turns out that the girl was dead set on the M word. Within a few minutes of having actually met and ordered appetizers, she started asking me about what kind of house that I wanted to live in and what kind of names I liked for kids and I just about choked on the breadsticks and was so desperate to leave Suzy Homemaker behind, I had Stan call me on my cell and left because of a "work-related emergency."

I still can't quite figure out what a "work-related emergency" would actually be for a guy like me. It's not like I'm a lawyer or a paramedic. I guess I could always make up some sort of weird excuse. In a city like Ottawa, someone's always needing some paper or report or letter or some piece of paper that will unlock the mysteries of bureaucratic nightmares all over the world. Those are the things that deputy ministers call people up at midnight for. They're so vague and weird anyway, who would really think to question that? In any case, I made my getaway and have not called whatever her name was and I'm sure that she's since roped in some other guy into the kind of house that she wanted and with the right kids names.

I work downtown in one of the ugly office towers built in the 1970s which were the reigning years of asbestos and cheap concrete. The building is a drab brown colour that is forgettable and muddy and actually looks downright shitty in freezing February. The office itself is on one of the upper floors, but all the windows are occupied by management, so none of us working joes really enjoy the view. The office always smells of a medley of carpets, ink and stale coffee.

We get to file into packed light grey cubicles with the soft walls and absolutely no sound barrier or privacy, with just enough room for a desk and chair and maybe a few cabinets if we're lucky. It's a pretty dull atmosphere, but most Ottawa government building are entirely soulless, so it's really no surprise.

So, anyway, I got into work that Monday morning and it was freaking freezing outside and I hadn't pulled out my jacket since I was still naively holding onto the thought of summer, so I had to really haul ass to get from my toasty warm car into the office and of course, the first person that I had to run into was Don Juan Paul. There he was, walking in big long strides, probably so that his cock would have plenty of swinging room in the pants of his designer suit, a grin the size of Texas on his face. I tried walking ahead a bit faster so that he wouldn't buddy up to me, but I didn't quite make it and just as I was approaching the revolving door into the building, he landed a hard one right in between my shoulders, almost knocking my face into the glass.

"Hey, Gordie boy, how was your weekend?"

"Over now. How was yours?"

"Oh, you know how it is with me, Gordie boy. I've been back and forth a few times and hardly had a chance to get some shut eye with all the action that I've been getting. It's tough out there with so many women and so little time, you know?"

I'd like to smack that shit-eating grin right into the revolving door and watch it spin for a few cycles like laundry in the machine.

That's a nice thought, actually. I'll hold onto it while we get into the elevator.

"Hey, man, what's up?"

Adventure Tim makes it to the elevator right before it closes. As usual, he always makes an entrance, sliding in at the last possible second, almost getting squeezed in the metal doors like an accordion. He's got the goggles tan on his face, all red except for just around the eyes. The redness of his face is a pretty familiar sight, since he's usually off skiing or boarding or climbing or fighting off bears with his bare hands while on a nature trail somewhere. The redness is supposed to be part of his healthy look, like his long blonde hair.

He has that granola sort of sensibility to him and I think that granola makes up the bulk of what he eats and how any guy can get so massive on a granola diet is a mystery to me. He also eats handfuls of nuts in the office and I can always hear him from my cubicle. The crunching of nuts, combined with the beep of fax machines and photocopiers and listening to Cheryl talk to her friends over the phone about her divorce from the other end of the cubicle hall, all combine to give me an exclusive sneak preview of what hell must be like.

"Hey, man, check this out. You won't believe who I'm going to be seeing this weekend."

Don Juan Paul gives me a little wink that would get most people punched. I don't know how I hold myself back from decking him about twenty times a day. I must be a lot more patient than I give myself credit for. He pulls a magazine out of his coat pocket and opens it to an advertisement that features a tall, leggy, topless blonde holding a hose and wearing an open fireman's jacket. I have no idea what the product being advertised is. Nobody cares. Adventure Tim whistles. Don Juan Paul looks at me for my approval, so I smile and nod. This is how I get through most of my days.

Don Juan Paul makes his way over to his cubicle and Adventure Tim nudges me.

"He serious?"

"You never know with Paul. He might have an actual date with her or he might be jerking off to the photo later on. But I've seen women around Paul and it wouldn't surprise me one bit if she were hot and real."

"Fuck."

"Yeah."

"How does he do it?"

"I don't know, man. He's got a way."

"I didn't think women fell for that shit."

"Women fall for a lot of shit."

"Guess so. Hey, how's your girl doing these days?"

"Aw, we broke up. She left. Stupid fight."

"Tough, man. You think she's coming back?"

"Nah. I'm pretty sure she 'aint."

"Oh well. To hell with her."

"Yeah. You still going with that Swedish girl you met while mountain biking in the Alps?"

"Nah, she wanted to go back home and be with her family. One of those types. Can't take the wandering lifestyle. But I met this awesome Norwegian girl while snowboarding in Whistler. You gotta take up a sport, bro. It's the best way to meet the best women. They're fit, competitive, tough. And a lot of fun. Up for anything. That's the way to go. None of these domesticated types who want to redo the bathroom and take the kids to soccer practice. You know what I mean? That's just a trap. Boring. Stiff."

"I hear you, man. If I could, I would. But I think I'll stick to watching sports."

"You watch too many sports, bro. Your head's going to go one of these days."

"Yeah, maybe. But you know how it goes, there are those that can and those that watch."

"It wouldn't take much. You could start out small."

"Yeah, I don't think so. Anyway, no girl's going to go for that guy that falls on his ass while skiing through trees."

"True."

"Got lunch plans today?"

"Nah. Where you want to go?"

"Deli across the street?"

"Noon?"

"Yeah."

"Okay."

I get into my cubicle and turn on my computer. I have one of those cubicles that hasn't changed since the day that I moved in. There are no decorations, no pictures, no cute posters with witticisms on it, no sign that a person actually works there. While some people take it upon themselves to pretty up or personalize their work space, I'm of the opinion that I'm there to work and that I want to spend as little time there as possible, so it just needs to be a place where

I hang out from 9 to 5. There are other people in the office who have their second home in their cubicle with pictures, posters, toys, a whole separate wardrobe sometimes and a grocery store in their filing cabinet. I don't do any of that stuff. If it wasn't for the plastic nameplate, you'd think the office was vacant. Oh, how I wish.

As usual, my inbox is over its size limit and half of the stuff that's come in over the past couple of days are dirty jokes sent to me by other cubicle friends. I spend a couple of hours filtering through the crap and then my boss walks by my office three times, wondering whether or not to actually nail me with the work while I'm sitting there looking half alert. My boss is one of those middle-aged, medium height and build guys with ambiguous features, glasses, and slightly metrosexual tendencies. He sometimes wears colours that men don't typically wear and loud prints that make no sense. He's straight-laced and always wears a shirt and tie. I don't think he even owns jeans.

He comes in and gives me something to finish for noon and I get started on it while Cheryl in the cubicle next door sobs into the phone and goes over the latest details of her nasty divorce from a guy that she married 17 years ago at the age of 20 and who has since left her for a woman who is, guess what?, 20.

Adventure Tim is browsing various websites for more extreme adventures to take and Don Juan Paul, still with that shit-eating grin on his face, is texting someone or several someones on his phone, probably going over lurid panty details from previous nights. Then John, one of the pathetic marrieds from accounting, wanders over to talk to me about sports. I always feel like I have to give him a few minutes of my time, even if there's work on my desk, since the poor guy's so whipped by his wife that he may as well wear his frilly apron to work and I think that talking sports with me is his only way to remind himself that he wears the cock.

At noon, I head out to the deli with Adventure Tim and he orders some sort of soggy wheat germ soya sandwich thing and I grab a smoked meat sandwich on rye loaded with mustard. He tells me about the canoe trip that he's going to take with a buddy of his and two girls and how they're going to go through rapids and canyons and camp all of the way for about 15 days in the wilderness. I have no idea how this man does it. He does everything seemingly with one hand tied behind his back. I have trouble sleeping in a motel and this guy's going to sleep in the woods under a piece of tarp which will be his only source of protection from wind, rain, lightning and bears. Fuck.

A half hour later, I'm back in the office and something else has landed on my desk and three more friends have sent me dirty jokes and one invite to a pub later on. Cheryl is now calling up her third or fourth support friend of the day to talk about her divorce and keeps going on about how she needs a spa day or something to treat herself and I just want to yell over the goddamn wall to go on the freaking spa day, I'll even pay for half of it, just get the hell out of the office and stop crying in your goddamn soup, the man's a piece of shit and she should just get on with her life.

One of the cute girls comes down from HR at around 2 in the afternoon to talk to Adventure Tim about something that he needs to fill in and Don Juan Paul takes full advantage of the situation to go over and ask Tim about some important "item of business" which means that he desperately needs to know what her cup size is. The girl, whose name escapes me for some reason, is one of those giggly types that always dresses for nightclubs, even in the office. They wear the midriff tops and the too short, too shiny skirts, but nobody ever calls them on it, the guys, because they like to look, and the women, because they don't want to be called stuffy old bitches.

So once she's done with Tim, Don Juan Paul starts to make his moves and gives her the lines and she's smiling and flipping her hair over her shoulder as if she's on the set of some sappy soap opera and he's leaning over the cubicle wall with his arm out as if he's at a cocktail party and she's just eating it all up. Tim rolls his eyes at me; I put on headphones.

By the time that this dreary, predictable spectacle is over, Don Juan Paul's got another date and phone number and he's walking back to his cubicle with the swagger of a guy who's grown another testicle. My boss comes in to let me know that he'd like me to stay late, since he suddenly got some new work for me, which, if he had given it to me an hour ago, would have meant that I would not have had to stay late in the first place and now I have to email my friend and let him know that I'll be about an hour late to meet him at the pub but will still make puck drop and I'm swearing under my breath as Tim and Paul leave on time while I'm stuck making corrections to some crappy report that is going to sit on the corner of someone's desk for 3 months before someone picks it up. Fuck.

So I pull this shit together and get out of the office just as the cleaning guys come in to empty the garbage cans. I race to the elevators, get to the pub which is crowded, only to find that my friends have all started without me and I'm going to have to order food right away or I'll be eating alone. The waitress avoids me every time that I try to get her attention, so I give up and head to the bar to get my drink and get stuck behind some blonde on her cell phone as she discusses her new boyfriend at a high volume and talks about how rich he is and what kind of car he drives and I wish that I could shove her someplace, but guys don't do that kind of thing, so I just glare at the back of her narrow head.

The game's great, but it's not my team. Still, it's hockey. The waitress finally gets it together and brings me a platter of wings with barbecue sauce and a mess of fries. She looks appropriately bored as she brings it, like one of those pretty girls that decides she's going to wait tables while waiting to be discovered and move on to a supermodel career. She's cute, but in that bland way that most of the nameless girls that you see in clubs are, the ones that you see by the dozen and who have fairly generic names like Laura or Jessica.

The food's not bad. Some of the guys try flirting with the waitress. They always think that this is the way to go and that they're actually going to get her to smile. Doesn't work. I could have told them that.

Freaking Monday.

Chapter 12—Tired Tuesday

I'm always tired when I come in on Tuesday because of the night that I had on Monday. It's kind of a vicious cycle thing. But when you know your Tuesday looks identical in content to Monday, it really doesn't make a difference if you're tired or not. At least not where I work.

I sit back in my chair, alone with my thoughts, with the odd ringing of the phone or the constant hum of the photocopier in the background. I've surfed the web about as much as I can for one day and I'm slowly feeling lethargic or melancholic, up until the point that they seem like exactly the same thing. I've finished lunch and my coffee and there are no more distractions until that hand hits the 5, so I lie back in my seat as far as I can without falling over and think.

This is generally the day that I have those long stretches of time in the late afternoon to think about my life and what went wrong with it. It's a sort of mini existential crisis. Who am I? Where am I? How did I end up here? Why am I working this dead end job instead of hanging out at the Sports desk on TSN, making predictions, running off scores, playing the fantasy pool and arguing about the latest draft picks? Is this all there is to life? Wouldn't I be happier raising cabbages? What is the problem with women? Am I the problem or are women just crazier than they used to be?

Of course, I know that most of the guys who are lucky enough to work in sports are the guys who are either really well-connected or are former sports stars themselves, so it makes sense that this is not a world that I can easily get into without starting at the bottom and getting everyone's coffee. There are days that I think that it would all be worth it; then there are the days that I'm too chicken shit to do anything drastic that would change my life because I've gotten so comfortable in my rut, picking up my paycheque at the end of the day and grabbing lunch down the street.

So what's the answer? Should I just marry the next girl who comes along and hobble through life with some kids on my back? If I was meant to be that way, wouldn't I have proposed to Miranda? She would have been a nice wife. She was a pleasure to live with. She took care of everything, she cooked meals, she did laundry, she put up with me sitting on the couch while watching Sports Centre every night, she did all of our banking. I don't know why I didn't marry her. As sad as it may be to say it, I just don't think that I felt like bothering.

It's strange when you have these little crises. You can usually figure out what went wrong, but it's almost impossible to figure out what to do about it.

"Hey, Gordie. Look alive."

I looked up in time to catch a softball coming towards my head. Adventure Tim was standing in front of me. It was already the end of the day.

"Been trying to get your attention for the past 5 minutes, you are totally zoned out like a pothead. Let's go, working day is done and done. Let's go grab a burger and a beer."

Best suggestion I've heard all day.

Chapter 13—Weak Wednesday

Wednesday in the world of the public service is only good twice a month. The reason for this? That's the day that we get paid, every two weeks. We usually celebrate that occasion by taking an extra long lunch over at the pub and having a pint even though it's the middle of the day and we all have to trudge back into the office for the afternoon. I used to object to drinking during the workday because I wasn't sure if I would (a) stop (b) say something objectionable, like telling my boss to fuck off or (c) be too happy to actually work. Since then, though, I've relaxed a lot. This is mostly because I've realized that work is never going to be either interesting or challenging, so it doesn't matter if I've had a beer or not. I've also learned that one beer won't induce me to tell my boss to fuck off and so I feel safe on this one.

Unfortunately, this is not one of the good Wednesdays. This is the weak one where you wish that it was the other one. It's like going on a date with the friend of the girl that you wanted to go on a date with. Weak Wednesday.

John comes towards my cubicle. He's one of those guys with hooded, drooping eyes behind Coke glasses, a thinning hair line and a small pot belly stomach. Everything about him is soft and harmless. His wife buys his clothes for him, and he spends his weekends checking off items on his wife's to-do list. He has three children, two daughters and a son who's in high school. His dog Biscuit is a big black and white mutt that he rescued from a shelter several years ago and he's one of the most docile family pets that you've ever seen.

John wanders over to my desk with a cup of coffee in his hand and a piece of paper in the other. The cup has a picture of his daughter and their dog, Biscuit, on it. It was a gift from his wife. The piece of paper is a fax that he picked up off the fax machine. It's an ad for low rates for Vegas.

"Have you seen this?," he asks.

"No. Where did it come from? We always get those travel deals on our fax machine and I can't figure out who's sending them."

"The travel companies. Taking advantage of their government accounts and of bored desk jockeys like ourselves. You ever been?"

"Once. Bachelor party weekend for my best friend."

"Really? What was it like?"

"It was pretty crazy. It's a chaotic place, lots of lights and high-rise hotels. Girls everywhere in their skimpies. Lots of strippers. You know, it was a bachelor party. I'm sure you had the same?"

"I didn't get a bachelor party. The wife didn't think it was a good idea. Anyway, the guys I knew, they weren't into that kind of thing. It's something that I wonder about, though. I would have really liked to have had one wild guys weekend, you know? Well, you're still single and wild, aren't you?"

I can see in his eyes that he's one of those guys who believes what he sees on television about single guys. I can see that he believes that I'm one of those guys in the deodorant commercials, doing extreme sports and bedding lots of girls in clubs. I know that this isn't true, but how can I disappoint a guy whose life has become a domestic cage and who wasn't even 'allowed' to have a bachelor party? He looks at me with his eyes shining, his lips poised over his homemade cup with his daughter and Biscuit on it. I can't break this guy's bubble. I'm just not made that hard.

"Yeah, well, you know."

He nods. He knows.

My boss wanders in after John walks off. He enters my cubicle and perches himself on the edge of my desk, one of those classic boss moves that everyone hates. They sort of do it to make you feel like they're your buddy, but all you can think about is the fact that your boss' ass is on your desk. He sits down and starts to explain a new assignment to me, making judicious use of his hands to demonstrate things that my poor brain may not understand, such as opening his hands to indicate a report and making a writing motion to show me that he wants me to write the report. All I can do is stare at his tie which is bright pink. I can't believe that I'm taking orders from a man who wears a pink tie. That's like working out with Richard Simmons.

When he's done explaining my new work assignment, I nod to let him know that I've understood. He then makes as if to leave my cubicle, hesitates at the door, and then very casually mentions that he'd like to have the first draft on his desk by the end of the week. Then he and the pink tie disappear and I have to stop myself from banging my head on the part of the desk where his ass just was.

Well, I know that I've got a ton of work ahead, but given the sight of the tie, I decide to wait it out a bit with a quick break to check out some scores on TSN's site. I work better under pressure anyway.

I have been to a bachelor party weekend in Vegas, but the greatest bachelor party weekend that I've ever been to was in Toronto. It was years back before Roger turned into an idiot on his wedding day. We took him on a road trip to Toronto and rented two cars so that we could all go, his brothers and cousins included. They were a tight crew, great guys and like all Irishmen, good drinkers.

We stayed in a large suite at a nice hotel downtown, spent a day at the Hockey Hall of Fame, had our pictures taken with the Cup (they even let us touch it, fulfilling all my childhood fantasies), took in a baseball game and went to some of the best restaurants in town, chowing down on the greatest ribs and steaks. We even managed to get some ridiculously priced scalper tickets for a Leafs game where we drank beer and heckled the losing Leafs to, well, a loss. We almost got beaten up when we left. It was an unforgettable night. Luckily, Roger's cousins were also 6 foot 6, so they prevented things from getting really crazy, otherwise, we would have come home black and blue.

That was my favourite Bachelor party weekend of all time. Even when it looked like I was going to get my ass kicked and I was too drunk to care, I can't help but think about that moment and laugh. I wouldn't have changed a single thing about that weekend. The only thing that I wish about that weekend was that there were more of them.

Chapter 14—Thirsty Thursday

"You know, I was talking to this guy in the office the other day and he was telling me about bachelor parties and how he never got one and you know what I started to think about? You remember that awesome bachelor party weekend we took in Toronto years back?"

"The one where you almost got your ass kicked by the Leafs fans? I remember that one, how can I ever forget? That's the same trip where we lost Mark at the strip club."

"I thought we lost Mark at the strip club in Vegas."

"No, I remember we lost him in Toronto. It was that really weird dive and we were wondering if we should leave because there was that gang that came in at 2am and Dan said that I was racist to call them a gang just because they were a bunch of black guys but they were all wearing the same jacket, so they were either a gang or a boyband and it had nothing to do with them being black."

"Oh yeah. How did we lose him anyway?"

"I don't know. We were all having a good time and when we got the cab to get back to the hotel at 3am, nobody knew where he was."

"Where did he spend the night? I just remember that he was in the hotel when we came back from breakfast the next day, but not how he got there."

"I don't know. The gang probably thought he was some kind of clown and threw him into a dumpster in Chinatown. He smelled like cabbage."

"Oh yeah."

"Those were some good times."

"Yeah, you know, I almost wish that some poor sucker we know would just get married so that we could throw him another bachelor party weekend. Wouldn't that be awesome?"

"Why do we have to wait for some poor sucker to get married? Why can't we just go one weekend? We can go on a long weekend and just blow this dead end dump."

"Georgie boy, that's the best damn idea that I've heard you have in years. But what about Paula?"

As if on cue, Georgie's phone rang and it was Paula. It was another Thursday in the pub straight after work with the guys and we were all sitting around in a booth with a pitcher of beer talking over the good old days. Business Dan had his Bluetooth on, but wasn't talking into it. He looked tired and apparently business was bad at the moment. He tried to explain it to me but I really didn't get it. Something about the market index or whatever that was killing people.

Stan was sitting back in the booth with his arms spread out, looking up at the ceiling, blissfully quiet in his corner. Roger was slouched over his beer and you could tell that he was lost in nostalgia too, remembering his time before he destroyed his life. Georgie left the table to get into another argument with Paula who was demanding to know where he really was and who he was really with. It was just another typical Thursday night out.

"That's a good idea, though," said Roger, looking up for the first time since the discussion got started. "We used to have a lot of fun together and it doesn't make sense for us to be all rotting here. We're single and young. We shouldn't be sitting around waiting for things to happen."

"Wow, that was like the last thing that I ever expected to hear from you, man. I could see someone saying this, but my money wouldn't have been on you."

"Yeah, well, it's time to stop waiting around for things to happen and just grow a pair."

"It's good to hear you say that. What happened, man? Did you meet someone?"

"No. I didn't meet someone. I haven't had that transformative love thing happen to me. My ex-wife's sister called. The little lady's getting married to some guy that she met while she was on a trip to Portugal with the girls and she wants to make sure that I'm not going to make trouble. Portugal. The trip that we were supposed to take for our honeymoon. She took off anyway with her little girlfriends and she's gone and married a Portuguese that she met out there. Some suave little fucker, I'm sure. Saw some heartbroken loaded broad on vacation and probably romanced her with all sorts of bullshit. Fucking unreal."

"Hey, man, that's good news. That means that you can get your apartment back up to bachelor pad status and we might actually come over once in awhile."

"Fuck you, Stan."

"Hey, just trying to look on the bright side of things, man. You're free. Really and truly free. Isn't it a good feeling?"

"Yeah, I guess it has to grow on me."

"You're going to love being a free man, Roger, my man. There's nothing better. Look at old Georgie. You want to become like that? Look, he's still on the phone, having the same argument with that dumb bitch wife of his. You really want your life to be like that?"

"I wouldn't trade places with Georgie, that's for sure. Paula's a nasty bitch. And she's not as hot as she used to be."

"Don't let her catch you saying that."

"Maybe I should, just to give her something to think about."

"Dude, you are so not drunk enough to be doing that right now."

"Maybe I should get it started then."

"That's alright with me. Hey! Another pitcher here."

"You know, I think that we should celebrate your newfound sense of freedom, Roger. I think, that instead of celebrating a man's sudden ball and chain arrangement, we should be celebrating freedom instead. The world's run all wrong, man. It makes no sense for us to celebrate something which is a goddamn shame. Goodbye to your good life, man. Goodbye to your carefree days. Goodbye to your balls, your wife's going to carry them around in her purse from now on and take them out only on special occasions. Fuck that. Really. We should be celebrating your freedom!"

"Freedom!," Stan gave us his best Braveheart impression with his glass in the air.

"Freedom!" echoed Dan. His eyes looked a bit glassy and I suddenly couldn't remember how many pitchers we had had anymore. In any case, it didn't matter, I was on a roll. I got up and stood on my chair. The waitress sent me a nervous look and the bartender sent me a look like I had just arrived to pick up his daughter for a date in my condition.

"We are NOT going to have a stupid Bachelor party weekend to recognize the end of your life! We are going to have a breakout weekend away to celebrate your freedom and the beginning of a new and improved life!"

"Hear, hear!"

"We are going away! No women, no job shit, no fucking Bluetooth crap, yeah, that's you, Dan. We're going to drink, we're going to gamble, we're going to see strippers, ballgames, steaks and forget shit! That's what we're going to do! And—don't worry man, I'm almost done, I'll get down in a second, it's cool, it's cool—we're going to have the best time ever! And the best part is? Nobody has to be sacrificed so that it can happen!"

"Yea!"

We all clanked glasses and cheered. Even guys who weren't with us started to come over to toast with us. The bartender was still giving me the stink eye, so I grudgingly got down from my chair and started toasting everything in front of me, the ketchup bottle, the mustard, the napkin dispenser. The waitress was really starting to look nervous now, like she was afraid to make eye contact with us or something. Georgie came back to our table and noticed all the other random people there and the sudden festive air.

"What did I miss?"

It was so damn funny. We couldn't help but laugh ourselves stupid. Poor Georgie kept looking around for someone to fill him in on the joke, but we were too busy pissing ourselves to explain it to him. Finally, Stan stumbled over and put his hand on his shoulder.

"We're going away for a guys weekend. You're coming with us."

"Well, I'd love to, you know, but I gotta clear things with Paula."

"Don't worry, man, we'll clear things with Paula."

"Shut up you drunk assholes. I'll figure something out."

"Let's call her now."

"Yeah, dial up the ice bitch. Let's tell her you're leaving with us."

"Are you out of your mind? She already thinks that you're a cover story for some ass on the side, don't go making things worse by trying to talk to her. Anyway, I wouldn't trust you guys to talk to a toaster in your condition."

"I'll have you know that I can outtalk a toaster any day of the week."

"Come on, don't be a pussy. Call up the old nag and we'll tell her what's up."

"Get the fuck away from me, man."

"I'll do it myself. I'm not afraid of her."

"What the hell—hey! Hey! Don't you do it, Stan, don't you fucking dare!"

Stan was just too quick for Georgie and he caught him by surprise. He had Georgie's cell phone in his hand and he was loading up the speed dial. Georgie was trying to get to him, but Stan's a good head taller than Georgie and he was keeping him off with one arm while using the other arm to hold the phone. We all watched in amazement. The phone started to dial.

"Put in on speaker!" yelled Dan.

"Oh my god, the crazy fucker's actually calling her!"

"Hello?"

You could hear a pin drop in the pub. Everyone had gone dead silent. The random guys at our table were all slack-jawed in anticipation of hearing the ice bitch talk. Even the bartender looked interested now. The waitress was staring at us in horror, as if we had all grown three heads. Stan was holding the phone an arm's length away from Georgie who had suddenly frozen in place. His face was red with rage and embarrassment, but he couldn't even utter a peep. We all held our breaths and waited for Stan to say something.

"Hello? Who is this? George? Where are you? Oh my God. Oh my God. Don't tell me. A silent caller? You're totally the slut that he's screwing on the side. Is that it? You totally called so that you could hear my voice. Well, hear this bitch! That's my man you're dealing with and there is no way that I'm going to give him up without a fight! You hear me? I'm going to rip out your eyes, you filthy whore! Don't you even think of stealing him away! He is never going to leave me! You are worthless! You are the meaningless couch fuck in this relationship and there's no way that you're going to take what's mine from me! You hear me?"

"We hear you, Paula. Everyone here at the bar hears you."

It was like the whole room gasped at once. Georgie had gone from red to white. He was standing there with his eyes closed. The other end of the line went silent, as this was clearly not the voice that Paula had been expecting to hear. Stan then went on in a very calm, collected manner.

"We've been telling you for years that Georgie's out on the town with us and that's where he's always been. He's a good guy and he's never been a skirt chaser. Nobody knows why you think that. Nobody knows why you say some of the awful things you say. But now that we've all heard them, I think it's fair to say that you don't deserve a good guy like Georgie. And nobody understands what Georgie sees in you. I think it's time that this thing got settled once and for all. I think that in this room full of witnesses to your bad and irrational behavior, that you and Georgie should be separated. Ladies and gentlemen. We have gathered here today to witness the joy of freedom everlasting and to separate this man from this woman. Do you agree to this, ladies and gentlemen present, that this union should be annulled on the basis of what you have heard here today?"

He started off like Oprah and wrapped up like a Southern Baptist preacher. It was impossible not to be charmed.

"YES!" yelled the room, the bartender and waitress included.

"And do, you, Georgie, the blameless party to this wretched union, agree to this?"

"Yes," whispered Georgie. We all watched him, as he slowly pulled himself out of a daze. "Yes," he said louder.

"By the power invested in me, as witnessed by all those present, I now pronounce you man and separated wife! Good riddance!"

"Hear, hear!"

There were more cheers and more glass clinking. Then, the whole bar got silent again as we waited for a response from the other end of the line. We waited for a moment, anticipating a storm of backlash, a final stab from the ice bitch herself.

The phone clicked. We all cheered.

Georgie started to regain some colour in his face. He collapsed into the booth as if all the energy had been drained out of his system. He looked up at me from where he was slumped in disbelief.

"Gordie?"

"Yeah, Georgie?"

"Can I stay with you for awhile?"

"Sure, man."

"Thanks."

I don't remember how many drinks I had, but I'll never forget that night.

Chapter 15—Freedom Friday

"Georgie?"

"Yes, Gordie?"

"What are you doing?"

"What does it look like?"

"It looks like you're doing laundry."

"That's because I am doing laundry."

"What are you, my wife? Sit down."

"Ok."

We sat down on the couch in the living room in between three full baskets of laundry and it felt really weird. Like we were some gay old married couple. Georgie had been living with me for two weeks by that time, and I suddenly became aware of just how long it had been since I had lived with anyone. I was really used to my own time and space and having it occupied by anyone was just plain weird. The first week was ok, mostly because I still had a lot of sympathy for Georgie after that glorious night at the pub, but also because it felt temporary. Now I wasn't sure how long he'd be there and didn't have the heart to ask.

Georgie was a good roommate, though. Everything in my apartment got fixed and there wasn't a single leak or loose screw to be found anywhere. I think he even managed to fix my closet door. He tried to do a lot of things so that he could feel like he wasn't mooching, but the thing is, I didn't really mind him being there. Just as long as he didn't act like my wife. I just wanted him to be himself and sit on the couch and not fuss with stuff or try to talk to me. It's really odd to find yourself constantly in the presence of someone else and I was clearly rusty when it came to my social graces.

"I ordered a pizza."

"Good."

"Did you talk to the guys about Roger's weekend?"

"Yeah. Dan's taking care of it. He's making the reservations and stuff. It's going to be a good one."

"I'll bet."

"Have you talked to her iciness this week?"

"Nah. I haven't talked to her or seen her at all since the big night. I don't know if I want to bother, really. As far as I'm concerned, I only have to head over if I want my shit back and I don't know if I want my shit back that badly."

"We can always get you new stuff."

"Yeah. I'll worry about it later."

"Ok."

I feel like I should talk more, but I don't really want to get into it. It feels like this part of the conversation is pretty much done, right? No need to keep it going? I looked at him nervously from the corner of my eye. Georgie was looking straight ahead, but his hands were drumming nervously on the arm of the couch. He cracked his knuckles.

"How's work?"

Oh God. The 'how was your day?' syndrome rears its ugly head back into my life.

"Sucks, man. Like it always does. You?"

"Same. Sorry, man. I don't know why I'm doing this shit. I feel like I need to talk dumb shit with you because you're around and I don't know why."

"Old habits. You're used to the 'honey I'm home' scene."

"I guess."

"You miss it?"

"Paula, man? No, she's a bitch. I should have left her years back. But I miss the being together thing. It kind of grows on you," he grins.

"I wouldn't know."

"Relationships. They change you. They make things different, but they can be nice. It does feel like you're involved in something, something that's not just you. Well, that's a shit stupid way of saying it, but you know what I mean."

"Yeah. I know what you mean. It must be a change."

"Yeah. Just a change."

"It will get better."

What else was I supposed to say? I had to say something. I couldn't just sit there on the couch pretending to be absorbed in the latest Swiffer ad. Georgie shrugged carelessly.

"I know. It's already gotten a bit better. Don't have so many headaches."

We laughed at this. The damn Swiffer ad ended and the second period began. The doorbell rang and the pizza had arrived. With relief, I got up to answer the door. Finally. I could enjoy my evening.

Chapter 16—Out of Town

It was time to go. The bags were packed, the tickets were booked and there was going to be one sweet suite waiting for us when we arrived in Toronto. Everything was mapped out for us: tours of the breweries, seats to the ball game, reservations for rib dinners, even a huge Hummer limo for when we hit the town and pre-paid bottle service at the club. Dan would have prepaid our lap dances at the strip club if he could. Did he? Wait . . . .

Georgie was sitting on the couch still, pretending to watch a documentary on the Serengeti.

"Georgie, what the fuck? Aren't you ready to go?"

"I'm going to stay here."

"The hell you are. We've been planning for weeks, man, we're prepaid, locked and loaded and there's a car downstairs."

"I don't feel well."

"What, you got your period?"

"Just back off. I just want to be alone and I don't want to go and bring the party down. You guys go on without me and have yourselves a good time."

Alright, it was time for an intervention. I grabbed the remote and turned off the documentary while the hyenas were in the middle of chasing down a zebra.

"What's wrong? For real?"

"I just want to be left alone. That's all."

"Is it because of the Paula thing? You're not going to sit around all weekend and think about it, are you?"

"Well, there's been a lot to think about. But no, man, I just don't want to go anymore. I'm not feeling it."

"Look, I know you're feeling down and stuff's been weird lately and I'm not a good person to talk to. I get that. But you're going to feel so much better if you just come out with us and let yourself go a little. Have some fucking fun. We all need that once in a while and I'm beginning to think that you don't even know what fun is anymore. Come on. We're going to have the best weekend and we're going to drink more beer, eat more ribs and see way more titty than we've ever seen before. It's going to be epic and you'll feel like a sissy bitch if you miss it."

"Hmm. I'll probably want to kick myself in the balls if I don't go."

"Hell, I'll do it for you."

"Tempting, but no."

"What?"

And then his phone beeped. And then the caller ID showed Paula. And then it clicked.

"Oh fuck no."

"It's not what you think, Gordie. She just wants to talk. I have to talk to her eventually. There are papers to get signed and I have all my shit at her house."

"You are kidding me, man. After all that we've been through to get you here, after all the shit that you took, you're actually thinking of reconciling with the icicle bitch of the East side?"

"I'm not reconciling. I haven't made up my mind. She's just coming over to talk."

"If you think for one bloody second that I'm going let you use my place to be the site of a reunion with the wicked freaking witch of the Eastern Sideboard, you have lost your everlovin' mind! There's no reconciling with that and you know it! How long will it be until all the sweet kissy face talk turns into more jealousy? How long will it be until you're walking around with your tail between your legs because you have a curfew and an allowance? Fuck that shit, man! You can't be doing this! I won't let you do this! Get the fuck off the couch, grab your stinkin' duffle bag and get the hell in the car!"

I don't think that I've ever talked like that to anyone before.

Georgie was impressed. Silent, but impressed. The phone beeped again and he looked at it for a minute. Then he looked back at me. Then he looked back at the phone. I was standing at the door with it wide open and some random teenage girl walked by with a basket of laundry, looking confused. She must have heard me.

She looked at me for a while before continuing down the hall. I don't know if she thought that I was crazy or not, but she had a nice look in her eyes, almost like she understood. Georgie turned the phone off, picked up his bag and walked up to the door.

"If I ever do this again, you will let me know, right?"

"I'll let you know, Georgie."

"Thanks, Gordie."

"Don't mention it."
We were on our way to the best weekend of our lives.

Chapter 17—It's all kinda blurry . . . .

OhmyGod I'mhaving the greatest time ever!
Everythingisawesome
everyoneisawesome
Ilovebeer
Iwouldloveanotherbeer
Ilovebeeranytime doesit makemealcoholic to love beer so much?
Why? Why? Why must everythinggoodbesobadforyou?

Iamaluckyman
Ihavethebestfriends
Iloveribs

Wait,IhavetogototheATM
Wait,Ihavetogotothebathroom
Wait,Idon'tknowwhatIgottodofirst

Aw, thanks Georgie, you don't gotta spend your last twenty bucks
on a lap dance for me . . .

Yeah,shedoeslooklikePaulaminustheicebitchiness

Baseballissofun!

Howdiditgetsohotinhere?

DidIlosemywatch?

SweetCaroline!BahbahbahsomethingsomethingwordIdon't
know . . . .

DidImakeoutwithamaninadressatthatgaysingalongbar?

Iswearhelookedjustlikeagirl . . .

DidhereallysayIkissnice?

Where'sStan?

DidweloseStan?

Theseeggrollsarefantastic!

Ikissnice!

MyslapshotisWAYharderthanYOURslapshot!

IhavenoideawhatIjustdidthere

Ican'tbelievethosejeanscost100bucks

Yeah,yourasslooksgreat

CanIblowthewhistle?Isitmyturntoblowthewhistle?

Hey,itistruethatyouguysallgotfiredfromSleemanandthenhadtogeta
newjobwithyourmicrobrewerything . . . whybusinesspeoplegottago
andfuckthingsup . . .

Where'sStan?

ItissofuckingHIGHupintheTower!

Beerbeerbeerbeer

No,man,I'mnotTHATkindofguy,Idon'tjustgointobarsandmakeoutwi
ththegirlintheshortestskirt,Idon'tdothatshit . . . .

Oh,youthinkthatICAN'Tdothatshit?Really?Really?Ohyeah?Ohyeah?

I'msogonnagetbeatupagain . . .

Where'sStan?

Ikissnice!

Justletmesleepacoupleofmoreminutes . . . .

Whywon'ttheroomstopspinning?

Ilikehashbrowns

Where'sStan?

HowdidIhurtmyhand?

Wheredidthisbruisecomefrom?

HowdidIgetsomuchlipstickonmyface?

Whatthattasteinthebackofmymouth?

Dude,whathappenedtoyourface?

Wouldn'titbefunifwestoletheCup?

Ah,let'snot.

Whatyoulookingat?

Youcan'tthrowmeout-Ihaven'tdoneanythingandI'mnotfromaroundh
ere-no,man,becool,don'tthrowmeout . . .

OhmyGod.Imaybebannedfromthehockeyhalloffame.

Where'sStan?

Whycan'tyoufinddecentpoutineat2aminToronto?

I'mgonnabesick

YOUmakemesick!

Uhoh . . . .

IthinkIneedtosleepnow

What'sthatringingsound?

What'syourname?

Where'sStan?

Tequila!

Wait,whosetequilaisthis?

IsthatMexicanmusic?

Holasenoritas . . .

Badidea . . . .

Ikissnice.

Iamawesome!

Idon'twanttopackitup . . . .

Wheredidallmyunderweargo?

I'mjustgonnasleepinthecar . . . .

Wait,where'sStan?

Fuck . . .

Chapter 18—We lost Stan

Somewhere in all of our adventures, we lost Stan. Nobody's really sure how, but then again, we're not entirely sure he was with us for the entire trip. In any case, we did ask around before we left and everyone tried to give him a call. We even checked out some of the places that we had been to, although, well, not everyone could go back to those places and not all those places were welcoming to us. By the time he called me back, he was very, very confused.

It turns out that we had lost him on our last night out and he was calling me from a Chinese laundrymart on the other side of town. He had woken up without his phone, pants or wallet and was wearing a yellow sleeveless top that said Lovely on it—obviously, not his. Someone had applied clown makeup to his face while he was passed out and I'm pretty sure the underwear he was wearing wasn't his either because it had a Hello Kitty on it.

We had started out the night having dinner in the distillery district at an old steak house and somehow, Stan had gotten into the wrong cab. He should have figured out he wasn't with us when they all started speaking Mandarin. In any case, Stan's a nice guy and whoever they were took a liking to him and invited him out on the town—on the other side of town. Stan, being a highly adaptable guy and usually up for a good time with whoever, decided that he may as well try it.

The rest of the story kind of gets confusing from there, but the general idea is that he got trashed, traded clothes with one of the girls, decided that it would be a great idea to wash his pants at 2am while walking by the 24 hour Laundromat in Chinatown and then had a makeover while he was passed out on the floor.

We found his wallet in the machine, but not his pants.

I would have laughed out loud if I wasn't so damn tired.

Chapter 19—Poke my Eyes Out

It took me a week to recover.

I walked around like a zombie baby, clutching my pillow and downing Tylenol like it was candy. I kept drinking Gatorade even though it hurt to swallow. My throat felt raw and everything smelled like stale beer. Georgie was in the same shape, so we just slept and didn't talk. We both knew how the other one was feeling. I kept lots of bread in the house, hoping that it would help things along. It didn't do a heck of a lot.

I took some time to assess the damage one day. I had lost my watch, torn a couple of shirts, and somehow managed to come home with only 3 socks. I had gained a weeklong hangover, a sprained wrist, a phone number, a 6 pack of Steamwhistle from our tour and a red tube top. Georgie had managed to come home with an eye patch and a G string.

I was out in the four figure territory for my week of debauchery. I had taken a week off work and a second week off work to recover, during which time I legitimately felt sick. But I was pretty happy.

Until that Monday rolled around and I knew that I would have to face reality. My reality. Just last week, I felt awesome about my life. I was getting into trouble, drinking lots of beer, making out with girls I'd never see again, pigging out on racks of meat. Now I was going back to that prison and the never ending list of reports and nonsense work. It made me want to poke my eyes out. If I grabbed a pair of thumbtacks and put them in my eyes, they would have to let me out of boring meetings, right?

We were in the kitchen, getting ready to face the hostile world. Georgie was sitting on a kitchen chair backwards with his arms resting over the top, the picture of ease. I looked at him while I buttoned up my shirt, which felt stiffer than usual. He said that I looked like I was getting ready to face a firing squad. It felt that way.

"Fuck."

"It's not so bad, Gordie. You just have to go in there and remember all the bills you have to pay for our trip."

"I guess that makes it kind of worthwhile, right?"

"Well, when you work a shit job, you have to give yourself a lot to look forward to. Don't worry, man. We'll do this all again sometime. And we're all free men now, right?"

"Right. You planning to stay that way?"

"Yeah. I'll talk to the icicle sometime this week. And then I'll think about moving out."

"You don't have to be in a rush. I'm not kicking you out the door, you know."

"I know. You've been a good friend."

"Apparently, I kiss nice too."

"You ass."

"That's what the dude in the skirt said. You know it's true. Kissing a guy is exactly like kissing a girl."

"It's also what that minor said."

"She was 18."

"She said she was 18."

"Oh."

We laughed, but I was straining to remember if that was true or not. It didn't seem like me. Well, neither did making out with a transvestite. Definitely not me. It was kind of nice to not be me for a while. To not be a good guy, always doing the right thing and trying to avoid embarrassing myself. I've been raised to be a good boy. I hate it. I really do.

Georgie gave me a ride into work, so it was nice to just roll in at 9. I did my best to avoid Don Juan Paul and Adventure Tim was out again, no doubt doing something dangerous and awesome. That left me with my crying cubicle neighbor and my boss, who had very considerately left a pile of things on my chair like a welcome home present.

I needed coffee.

That's all I really needed. The rest of the day passed in an uneventful haze, almost like I was there but not there. I seem to remember doing some light, senseless work. I edited a document that was so boring that I had to read every page three times to make sure that I wasn't glazing over. All I could really think about was how much I hated being there and making a mental list of all of the places that I would rather be instead, like glamourous destinations around the world or just plain old home on the couch. I then thought of jobs that I was glad that I didn't do, like picking up garbage or working in a daycare. It seems like I go through this just about every day.

Something popped up on my Calendar. It was a staff meeting. Fuck.

Armed with more coffee, a pen and my notebook, I headed to the small conference room around the corner for our shit stupid staff meeting. The meeting room had beige walls and pot lights that were always too bright, as if they were meant to keep us awake. It was one of those meetings where my boss would talk at us and we would all pretend to listen. Someone may actually say something interesting at some point, but depending on how close we got to quitting time before that happened, only half of us may be listening by then. It was a long shot, of course, so I always made my best effort to write things down, even if I couldn't care less about them, to give the semblance of being engaged.

"Hello everyone. I trust that you all had a good weekend? Great. So, getting right down to business, you'll see in front of you an agenda which outlines the things that we have to talk about today. There are a few new priorities for the coming weeks, and depending on how things shape up in the Minister's office, we might be on call for some special projects . . ."

Special projects. Pet projects for Ministers that are urgent. Overtime and lots of time spent fussing about details that don't matter. Where were those damn thumb tacks?

"So there may be a few items that will have to take priority over our regular day to day business, but as you know, I have an open door policy and you can always feel free to come by and talk to me about whatever concerns that you may have . . ."

Open door policy. The 'keeping it real' catch phrase for all 6 figure managers who like to pretend that they're still cool. The one that nobody wants to use because they know it's fake and because truth be told, everyone wants less contact with their boss, not more. But it sounds good coming out of their mouths, so why wouldn't they say it? It's an easy way to look interested, like when you send a text message to someone who you have no intention of ever seeing.

"Next, I would like to report that we've received word throughout the public service that there are to be cuts made to our operational budgets. All things such as office supplies and supplementary travel and training opportunities will be reduced and every effort will be made to be more cost-effective. This also applies to our hospitality budgets, which means that we will not be able to host or offer coffee at our outreach meetings and that office supplies should be used sparingly."

Sparingly? How does one use an office supply sparingly? I guess I could stop using pens . . .

"Finally, I'd like to thank everyone for all their hard work. It's really been a tough few weeks and it looks like things will not be easy in the future, but rest assured, your efforts are noticed and appreciated by everyone, especially me."

Praise. Praise in the office is always a bad sign. It means that nobody is getting a raise.

I know how all this works. Your boss only praises you when there's shit coming down the pipe. They know that you're going to be asked to put in a ton of overtime with no budget to back it up. They know that you're going to be asked to do more with less and that there may even be less people around to do it. Praise is cheap. And bosses only pour it on when things start to look bad.

"Gordon, may I have a minute of your time, please?"

I hate it when people call me Gordon.

"Sure."

"Come to my office."

I followed behind like I was heading to detention. Once inside, he closed the door. Also bad. At least his office had a window, where I could gaze out at the sky and pretend to trade places in my mind with the birds flying by. I sat down, facing the window, while he clasped his hands together tightly and leaned toward me, intently. Also bad.

"Gordon, I know it's been awhile since you've been with this department. You've done a relatively good job to date and it appears that you're well liked. You're a young, bright man and I'm sure that you have aspirations and plans for the future . . . maybe a house, a wife on the horizon? In any case, you don't need to share the details of your personal life with me. But I was wondering if you would be interested in an acting position?"

"An acting position?"

"Yes. One year. We have a spot open since Mallory accepted a position with another department. She's announcing it today, her last day is Friday."

"Oh."

Mallory? The woman with the perfect nails who spent most of her day online shopping? She always had expensive designer brand clothing and accessories that she couldn't stop talking about. In truth, I had no idea what it was that she did. Who else thought to hire her? And what kind of mess did she leave behind?

"Of course, there would be a pay raise, roughly $15,000 a year that comes with the acting title . . ."

Money. Of course. Because titles don't mean anything in government unless there's money with them. But what the hell did she do? I can't remember what, if anything, she worked on. Why did he think that I could do the job? Of course, an extra $15,000 a year wouldn't be anything to sneeze at . . .

"Could I maybe think about it and tell you tomorrow?"

"Of course. Go home, think it over, talk it over with the wife . . ."

"I'm not married, sir."

"Oh . . . . right."

"Thank you for considering me for the opportunity, sir."

"Of course."

I walked back to my cubicle, feeling like I was made of lead. The good part of me, the 'Gordon' part, wanted to take the job because it was more money and it looked like I was doing something with my life, going somewhere and it would please my parents, particularly, my mother. The other part of me, which I'm not sure if it's good or bad, just didn't want to bother. I felt too mired in the office as it was, and I didn't want to get stuck any further. Taking the job might mean more hours and closer collaboration with my boss—two things that I didn't want to have in my life.

I made enough money. Sure, I could always make more. But is it always a question of money? Do we always need to make our decisions based on getting more of it? Then again, what would I really have to do to get it? Mallory was a bird brain and she somehow managed her job, whatever it was. It's funny how my boss hadn't even bothered to tell me what I would be doing. I guess that's also a bad sign.

Well, since I had no wife to talk it over with, may as well talk to the closest thing that I do have . . .

Georgie met me at the pub to talk things over a pitcher and some pub grub. It's easier to make decisions on a stomach full of chicken wings and deep fried zucchini sticks in sour cream. It was a mild fall day and we were basking in the sun out on a patio and life felt lazy and good. The urge to push thumb tacks into my eyes was gone, but the big question about the job was still bothering me just as much.

"What do you think, Georgie?"

"I don't know. It kind of sucks. You won't be making that much more once you pay taxes, you know."

"That's true. Do you think that I would have enough left over to buy some Sens tickets?"

"Now you're talking sense . . ."

"But then there are the cons. You know, overtime, working with my boss, doing stupid shit, going to more meetings . . ."

"Yeah, maybe the big wig meetings. They're even more boring from what I hear."

"How did this happen to us, Georgie? How did we end up here? Neither one of us ever wanted to finish up in office jobs. You wanted to be a mechanic and open up your own shop. Do you remember that? You could fix up any car."

"Yeah, I remember. But I had to get the real job for Paula. Fucking Paula. Fucking real jobs."

"Yeah, I remember that with Miranda as well. But I never got married. I never asked."

"Smart guy."

"Maybe."

"You're talking to someone who's about to be newly divorced, man, believe me, you are the smart one here. Man, that sounds weird."

"Yeah, you'll soon be a divorcé. How French."

"That just sounds gay for a guy."

"It does."

"I guess it's a good thing. Not looking forward to telling my mother, though."

"Tell me about it."

"You don't want to know."

"Well, at least you gave the whole marriage thing a shot, right?"

"Yeah."

"So what should we do? I mean, both of us. We're kind of both in a situation about now."

"We should find some twins and make out with them."

"Ok. After that?"

"I don't know. Maybe we should move in together."

"You proposing to me, big guy?"

"I can't, I'm in the midst of a divorce and it wouldn't be fair to you, sweetheart."

"Ugh. Don't ever call me that again. That gave me the chills. The bad kind."

"Alright."

"I guess it makes practical sense, though. My place is too small for both of us and it would be cheaper if we moved in together and split the rent. You're going to have to pay for lawyers sooner or later and I'm thinking that I need to have more interesting things to do with my life instead of work. And if we start splitting bills, we would probably be able to swing half season tickets to the Sens."

"You really got your priorities set, don't you?"

"You in?"

"I'm in."

"I guess I'll have to take that job to bring in more bucks?"

"It's up to you. Only if you want it. I don't think we'll actually need the money."

"I'll think about it some more. Overtime might make me late for puck drop."

"Or miss games entirely."

"That's unacceptable. The Sens look great right now. Don Cherry says it's gonna be Sens and Ducks this year."

"The Dirty Ducks."

"Yup."

"Well, you wouldn't want to miss that."

That was for sure.

Chapter 20—A Glimpse of Domestic Bliss

So it was all settled. I accepted the strange job offer that I didn't understand, replacing the scatty high heels who happily left the office with nothing behind, not even a memo to let me know what it was that I actually did. I spent the first week in my acting position in the HR department, hanging out with forms to sign and reading over my job description several times, trying to discern what it was that I was supposed to actually do. It was like trying to put together a jigsaw puzzle without the puzzle picture on the box.

My mother was thrilled. She thought that I was finally 'getting there', whatever that meant. I wasn't sure where 'there' was. Supposedly, it was my ultimate destination, but I've no idea where that is. It's a good thing that my mother has it figured out. It would be nice if she would share it with me.

Georgie and I moved into an apartment down the hall from mine, which had 2 bedrooms and a den. It was nice to have the den, actually, since we used it as a place to store our laptops and it was a good place to get away from each other without actually leaving the apartment. Georgie was easy to live with, to be honest, and I was lucky that we ended that way. I was just so used to my own space, it sometimes freaked me out to see things that weren't mine hanging around or coming home to find out that he was already there.

I actually think that the transition was easier for Georgie. He was used to having someone else around, although that someone else had pink things and smelled nice. But somewhere in the years, he got used to not being alone, and even though I didn't talk much, he didn't seem to mind that. He just seemed to like having someone else around. Maybe he needs a cat.

I'm deathly allergic to all things with fur on them, so that was out of the question. I would have to do in the meantime as his companion. We quickly fell into an odd couple sort of pattern. Coming home most nights, having dinner, talking about strange shit, and zoning out in front of the game. He knew what kind of pizza I liked and that I was all about the cheesy garlic bread on the side, and he always restocked the fridge when we were low on beers. Georgie's divorce proceedings started shortly thereafter, and he was gone a lot of nights in November, tied up in meetings with lawyers and icy conversations with Paula. I was there if he wanted to talk, but mostly he seemed happy to know that I was just there.

Work, meanwhile, was driving me out of my mind. We were just entering that grey dreary part of the year when it gets dark at 5pm and I was stuck in the office most nights, still trying to figure out what the hell it is that I do, and figuring out quickly that most of what I did was go to boring meetings and stay on call until 7pm most nights in case the Minister wanted something revised. That was my big promotion.

I could see now how Mallory had put up with her job. It was all the online shopping and the filing of her nails that kept her busy when she was on call. She knew that she would just have to put up with it a little while and it would only be a matter of time before her patience paid off. Basically, she wasn't anything special, but the fact that she stayed at her desk until 7pm every night in case someone needed something was what got her the promotion to another department—the equivalent of scoring airline tickets first class on standby.

This made getting tickets to the Sens games impossible, but it also meant that I could watch as many games as I wanted, because by the time that I left work, all I wanted were the same three things: the game, a beer and some dinner. Hockey had always been an important part of my life, but now, it was the basic focus of my life. When I got home, I was so brain dead and numb that I wanted to weep. I wanted to actually put my arms around the flat screen and weep with my beer in one hand.

And the Sens were WINNING. Not just winning. They were kicking ass. That was the only way to describe it. Spezza, Alfie and Heatley were on a tear this season and it looked like they were really going to take it all. They were also getting amazing support from Kelly and Fisher and while most people hadn't forgiven the Senators for giving up on Chara in favour of Redden, Redden was actually playing very well. They were an incredible team.

But then there was another painful reality attached to my promotion: weekends. My job actually required weekends. So I was forced to go in on Sundays during what my boss considered critical periods for the Minister. Not that anything happened on those days, so I never figured out what a critical period was. It just seemed like an excuse to suck the fun out of my life, which was what work was slowly doing.

I also got to know my boss in a whole new light. The man actually simpered. While he went around the office acting like a hot shot and talking down to just about everyone and everything in the office including the photocopier, he was an absolute nobody in all the important meetings. These meetings which made me wish for thumb tacks were the ones where he quietly sat in a corner, seemingly absorbing everything that was said and leading the rounds of applause every time there was some sort of achievement. There's always one person who has to do it and it looks like my boss was that person. He was, in short, a yes man on a power trip.

It was a low point in my life for everything social—I missed out on poker nights, my pool picks were all over the place because I hadn't had the chance to scope out my stats properly so my entire pool ran hot and cold during the season, the guys started to call me Mr. Important because of all my weekend shifts and Georgie even cracked a few jokes regarding my 'neglect' of him. And dating? I hadn't had a single date and wasn't even sure if I still knew what to do on one.

It was a high point in my life for my team—the Sens continued their tear on the league like Sparta's 300. I was so fucking proud, like I had something to do with it. It was also a high point in my life for something else: money. My new acting position was raking it in, along with the double overtime for my weekend shifts where I essentially sat around the office playing solitaire and reading sports blogs. And because I had zero time to flash my cash, it all stockpiled in the bank and made for some pretty awesome numbers by Christmas.

Christmas. Holy crap, Christmas was in a week and I had zero shopping done and had no idea where I was supposed to be on the big day. I supposed it was my mother's house for dinner. Holy crap. When was the last time that I talked to my mother? Had I really lost track of everything like that, being trapped in the office like an office slug?

I had no idea where the time went. It just seemed like every day was a repeat of the day before, stupid work, hockey game, Heatley, Spezza, Alfredsson, Georgie, takeout, beer, boring meetings, coming home late. And now months had passed me by and I had barely noticed. I guess this is what it's like to get old. They always say that the days, weeks and months just blur by together and it all happens so fast, that before you know it, you're another year older and wondering what the hell happened in the interim and it seems like everyone's getting married and having children and you can't remember the last time that you did anything fun.

Man. I was beginning to sounds like one of the marrieds. I guess this is what they mean by domestic bliss.

Chapter 21—It's Not a
Wonderful Life

It seems like every year, I end up watching *It's a Wonderful Life*. I don't mind it. It's actually one of the better Christmas films. It makes me wonder about whether or not things always turn out the way that they're supposed to. Here you have this guy who is just riddled with regrets because he never had the life that he had dreamed about as a boy, and yet, it turns out that everything turned out perfectly in the end and that he was perfectly blessed, just too thick headed to realize it until his guardian angel tells him so on Christmas Eve. It turns out that friends and family are more important than seeing the Taj Mahal or working a job that you actually like. I'm not so sure myself. It would be helpful to have a guardian angel to come down and figure it out for me.

The person who thinks that they have it figured out for me is my mother. She thinks she knows exactly what I should do and that's basically get somewhere in my career and settle down with a nice girl. It's the formula for happiness that just about everyone knows in Ottawa and seems to have. I guess I'm one of the freaky people who didn't get the memo.

My siblings did. My brother, Doug with his wife, Jenna, and two kids arrived at my mother's house an hour after I did. They had a boy and a girl, a year apart, two perfect carbon copies of themselves and they were now 4 and 5—great ages for yelling, running, and getting into lots of messes. They were also at that stage in their life where they thought that I was a bouncy castle, so they usually tried to bounce up and down on me while I tried to watch the game and made beer drinking impossible.

My sister arrived a half hour late for dinner with her husband and three kids, a set of twins who were 6 years old and a 2 year old boy who toddled after them, trying to be big. I felt the most for the 2 year old. He was the youngest, like me, and was always trying to play catch up. He wanted to do the things that everyone else did and didn't understand why he couldn't. And like me, he was obsessed with hockey.

Yeah, Tyler was my guy. Solid, light blonde baby hair and big blue eyes and constantly laughing. He was always batting furiously with the plastic stick and ball that I bought him for Christmas when he turned 2 and even though he was a small guy, he had a heck of good shot when he connected. He didn't quite talk in full sentences yet, so he would come up to me and point at me and then point at the ball.

"Gordie . . . hockey . . . . Gordie . . . hockey."

"That's my favourite song, big guy," I would say, and pick up a ball and stick to play with him on the floor. It seems like he was the only one in the family who got me.

I was in the middle of playing a second period with Tyler when my mother walked in. She sat down on the broken down couch in the basement and watched. Upstairs, everyone was listening to Christmas carols and drinking egg nog, which always made me think of snot. My father was wearing a felt red Santa Claus hat and pretending to feed the reindeers on the front lawn beer. He had obviously had a few himself. The whole house smelled of delicious food: turkey, steamed vegetables, mashed potatoes and rolls warming up in the oven. It was definitely the holidays.

"How are you, Gordon?"

"I'm fine, mom."

"No girlfriend this year to bring to Christmas dinner?"

"No. Just me and Tyler. We're a couple of old bachelors, up to no good."

"Always with the jokes, Gordon. It's a shame that you didn't get back together with Ashley. She was such a nice girl."

I honestly hadn't thought about her at all over the months. Why was she bringing her up? What was so nice about her? I couldn't remember any special details. I guess that's why she wasn't here.

"Well, you know I work a lot, mom."

"That's right, that's right. You don't have to work so hard, you know. You're still young, you have to have time to have some fun."

"That's what beer's for."

"Oh, son. You shouldn't talk like that, people will think that you're an alcoholic."

"People can think what they want to think."

"Seriously, son, have you thought about your future? The things that you want to have, other than hockey and beer?"

"No. I think that's all I want."

"Really?"

"Really."

"You don't really mean that, do you, sweetheart?"

"No, mom, I really think that I do. I'm a simple guy. I'm not hard to please. Things are going just fine."

She shifted on the couch, as Tyler let a slap shot rip towards my shin. He also farted loudly at the same time and broke out into giggles. I returned the shot back to him, remembering to do it softly so that he could catch up to it. It dribbled into the far corner and he waddled after it, laughing the whole time.

"What about your friend there? The one that's going through the divorce?"

"Georgie? He's ok. He doesn't talk too much about it, but it looks like things are getting settled. He expects to be fully divorced in a year."

"Did they have any children?"

"No, no kids. Roger didn't have kids either and his divorce just got finalized and his ex-wife remarried. Guess it doesn't pay to be in a rush, eh? That's two friends done before I've even made a trip down the altar. I think that I'm doing ok."

"Hmm . . . . I suppose so."

She made a clucking sound with her tongue that showed that she clearly didn't agree. Tyler whacked the ball dangerously close to where she was sitting and farted again. It looked like our conversation was about to end.

"Are you happy, Gordon? Truly happy, living your life like this? Being a bachelor, just going to work and drinking beer?"

"I don't know. I guess."

"Don't you want to do something more meaningful?"

"Like have children?"

"Well, yes, like have children. Settle down. Be in a committed relationship. Those are the things that add meaning to our lives, you know, not just sitting around and watching sports all of the time and only thinking about ourselves."

"Do I really seem that selfish and shallow to you, mom?"

"Of course not! I wasn't saying that. It's just that this life that you're leading right now just seems so directionless."

"So I should join EHarmony and volunteer in Africa?"

"Well, if that makes you happy."

"I doubt it. When's it time to eat?"

"Probably twenty minutes."

"Good. I'm starving. What about you, buddy? You hungry? You want to eat a big bird?"

"Big! Bird!"

That's my guy.

My mother rolled her eyes and then proceeded up the stairs to check on the progress of dinner. Tyler and I played out a third period where I let him win by a few hundred points, and then we made our way upstairs to have dinner. I grabbed a beer that I had been hoping for since I had arrived and we all sat down at the long table in the dining room. The table was set up with festive plates and those cracker things, but it didn't matter because the whole table was chaos. Tyler had crawled into my lap and my siblings were all over the place trying to fill plates for their kids as well as their own, while my father was pouring wine for everyone and my mother fussing about with pans and fancy spoons.

Nobody was paying attention to the spoons and were using whatever utensil was at hand to pile food on their plates and on their childrens' plates. My sister had her hands full with the twins and didn't even notice Tyler, who had settled himself happily on my lap and was helping himself to turkey on my plate, using both hands. He was getting greasy fingers and licking them. I shrugged and piled on more turkey.

"How is everything? Does everyone have what they need?"

"Yeah, yeah, yeah," from around the table.

I piled on some potatoes, stuffing and broccoli on my plate. Tyler attacked everything except the broccoli. I ate that first and then added more turkey, stuffing and potatoes. The gravy finally made its way to me and I poured it on top of the whole mess. Tyler made a second attack.

I had to give up at that point and just go for turkey with my hands while balancing my beer in the other. Tyler was dripping gravy by this point; the kid could've eaten from a trough and been perfectly happy. I looked around the table. All the other kids were just as messy and their parents were looking for washcloths. My parents were talking to my sister in law about something or other and they seemed absorbed in conversation. I was completely zoned out until my brother finally poked me.

"What?"

"I asked you the same question four times. Here. Take this."

I took the washcloth that he had in his hand and wiped off Tyler. He squirmed, but I managed to get him clean before he made another grab at the turkey left on my plate.

"What question was that?"

"You are totally a space brain, bro. I was asking about Ashley."

"Oh. Ashley's gone. We broke up sometime in September, I think."

"You don't even know?"

"It was a while ago."

"Oh."

"Yeah."

"What's been happening?"

"I took an acting position at work for a year. Got more pay and more stupid meetings to go to. It's been ok. A couple of my friends are getting divorced and I had a pretty fantastic guys week in October. Was a ton of fun."

"Sounds nice."

"You?"

"Same old. We redid the basement. You should see it. We made into a good rumpus room for the kids. They're going to have a lot of fun in it. Am also thinking of signing the kids up for baseball this summer."

"That's nice. They'll like baseball."

"I think they're finally old enough for T-ball. Jenna doesn't agree." He inclined his head towards his wife, still in deep conversation with our mother.

"Sports are good for kids. They'll be safe. They'll wear helmets."

"That's right."

"How about other things? Still in the same job?"

"Yeah, until I die."

He laughed, but it wasn't a serious laugh. It was a half choked laugh, like when he jokes about the old ball and chain. Jenna wasn't so bad, but she was a bit of a control freak. She liked everything to be the way that it should be and always wanted everything to happen a certain way. She asked a lot out of Doug, my brother.

"I guess it's always the same story."

"Yeah, well, we're govvies."

"Glad I'm not you."

"What, older?"

"Married."

"You jackass."

"Always have been, always will be."

"Well, enjoy it. Ride motorbikes. Go surfing. Do all the fun stuff while you still can."

"It's part of my plan, yeah."

"Well, don't wait. Because before you know it . . ."

I stuffed some more turkey in my mouth and took a good swig of beer while his voice trailed off and he rolled his head in the direction of my sister who was balancing a child on each knee while giving them a wipe down while my brother in law spotted Tyler and took him to the bathroom to change him. My guy was definitely loaded, but the good news is that he eats. Unlike some of the kids.

"Yeah, I know. So I've been told . . ."

We switched over the dinner plates and then dessert came. My mother had baked three different pies to go with everyone's preferences: blueberry, raspberry and pumpkin. The pumpkin was a bit of a strange sight, but apparently it's kind of a Christmas thing.

I dug into the blueberry and Tyler magically reappeared from the bathroom and settled his way back into my lap. My brother in law forced a plastic fork into his little hand before he could make a grab for the pie. It looked like dessert might be a less messy affair.

Just as my buddy and I were digging into the pie topped off with French vanilla ice cream, my sister in law showed up at my side, and the perky look on her face told me that she was up to something. Shit.

"So, Gordon, do you have plans for New Year's?"

"I didn't think of it, no. I'm probably just going to meet up with some of my buddies."

"Would you like to come to our party? We're just having a few friends over."

I sensed a trap. The party with single girlfriends who have recently broken up with someone and are looking for a nice guy kind of trap.

"Thanks, but I think I'll pass this time."

"Oh, come on. It will be fun! It will do you some good to see some other people."

"Some other people?"

"Other than just your poker buddies."

"You know that I hang out with them because I like them, right?"

"Oh, sure. But not all of the time. You have to get out and see new people once in a while."

"Thanks, but no thanks."

"Honestly, Gordon, I have no idea why you're so close-minded. Don't you want the chance to meet new people? It can be really fun and exciting."

"So can a trip to Fiji, but I don't have any plans for that either."

"You're such a stick sometimes."

"Well, that makes me really want to join your party now."

"Oh, you know what I meant, Gordon."

"You know that I hate to be called Gordon, right?"

"Oh?"

"Yeah. My actual friends call me Gordie."

"Oh. I always called you Gordon because your mother does. Does she know that you hate your own name?"

"Gordie is just more me."

"Oh," she sniffed.

I expected her to leave at this point, but for some reason, she didn't. She just kept sitting by my elbow, looking at me in that confused way, while I forked up more pie and stared straight ahead. Tyler's face was blue and he was smiling up at me.

"Do you plan to be single forever, Gordie? Are you an eternal bachelor type?"

"Maybe I am. Like Clooney. Awesome and single forever."

"I used to think that I would be single forever until I met Doug."

"Well, that worked out well for you."

"It might still work out well for you too if you just open up your horizons a little."

"Like if I do yoga and drink herbal tea?"

"Did you ever think that the reason why you don't have a girlfriend has to do with your attitude?"

"Sure."

She sniffed again, seeing as she clearly wasn't getting her point across. It was at this point that she decided that I was too thick headed to deal with and left. Tyler and I polished off a second helping of pie and ice cream and he slopped a big messy kiss on me before being carted away by my sister. He protested and howled as she bathed him quickly.

As the plates were being cleared, my father invited me and my brother into the living room for a night cap. He poured us each a big helping of single malt scotch and we sat down near the Christmas tree as it blinked on and off. The big meal and the conversation started to make me drowsy, and Bing Crosby's rendition of White Christmas playing on the stereo wasn't helping.

"What are your plans for the upcoming year, Gordon? What do you think you want to do?"

"I don't know. Watch the Sens go on a Cup run?"

"Other than that? What do you want to do for you?"

"I don't know. Maybe go skydiving."

"Don't be a smart ass, Gordie."

"I don't know. It sounds like fun."

I actually was interested in sky diving. And white water rafting. And ziplining. Why was that so weird?

"Fools risking their lives. And for what? To say that they've thrown themselves out of a plane? What good will that do you?"

My father, ever practical. Personally, I think that it might be a good idea to know that you can jump out of a plane successfully. There may be the odd situation in life where that would be useful.

"I hear you got a promotion at work. Congratulations."

We clinked glasses and drank. Not that I felt like celebrating that.

"I hear you got some friends going through tough times. Divorce."

"Yeah. It's rough. And expensive."

"People are so quick to get divorced these days. In my days, you stuck together, no matter what, and you didn't let life's little things get to you. Now people divorce because they don't like to see toe nail clippings on the bathroom floor. It's just ridiculous. People have to know what they're signing up for when they get married. It's not all flowers and wine. Real marriage is tough work. It takes choices, compromise, commitment. People don't seem to understand that these days, young people in particular . . ."

My father went on with his little speech, as he often does when he gets to the final nightcap at Christmas. It was the same speech that he gives just about every year, but he does have a point. It does seem like there are a lot of nothing divorces out there. Makes me never want to get married. Although Roger started to look a lot better since his divorce was finalized. He was finally beginning to relax a little bit and I think that he was actually dating someone last I heard. There was new life in him, yet.

I looked over at my brother, Doug. All of my life, my older brother had been a top athlete, bringing home trophies in basketball and soccer. He thrived on a super active lifestyle and got decent marks in school. He had a degree in accounting and worked in the Finance department of some other government organization. He used to tell me that he was going to get a job in sports, a dream very similar to my own. What the hell happened to us? How did we both get sucked into boring government jobs? And how did he get so old, married and settled? It actually looked like he was getting a pot belly and losing some of his hair. A lot of his hair, in fact.

"What?"

He noticed me looking at him. I shrugged.

"What was that job you always wanted to have when we were growing up?"

"I was going to be a sportscaster for the New York Knicks," he grinned.

"That's right. And I was going to be on SportsCentre. We were going to talk to each other on the show and share a condo in Toronto."

"Yeah. That was a great dream. We really thought we were hot shit at the time."

"And we were going to own a pair of BMWs."

"Mine was going to be a convertible, hard top. Red leather interior."

"Wow. You remember all the little details, too?"

"That one was pretty special."

"And we were going to cover all the big finals together and travel first class around the world and flirt with the prettiest stewardesses . . ."

"Interview athletes and get prime seats to big events like fight night . . ."

"And have the porterhouse steak . . ."

"And champagne and cigars . . ."

"Designer suits . . ."

"A couple of pretty assistants . . ."

"Vacations in Ibiza . . ."

"Maybe a maid and a cook . . ."

"Knuckleheads!"

Dad broke the spell, as he often did. He snorted at us and we stared into the bottom of our empty scotch glasses. Christmas was over.

Chapter 22—Margarita

The holidays were over and they weren't much to speak of. I hated the break from hockey games and New Year's Eve ended in predictable fashion, with me and the guys hanging around Stan's apartment and watching the SportsCentre top 100 plays of the year with a lot of beer and tequila shots. Despite the subzero weather, Stan barbecued hamburgers for everyone on his balcony, which was pretty cool of him. Then it was back to work and the same old grind.

Except for Georgie. Ever since he came back from spending Christmas with his family, he was strangely quiet. It kind of annoyed me when he talked so much when we first moved in together, but his not talking was even more off-putting. I wasn't sure what it meant. He wandered around the apartment a lot and started watching tv for hours, regardless of what was on. I knew that something was wrong when he started following American Idol.

I had no idea how to talk to him, though. I had no clue what was bothering him and even if he told me, I had no idea what I was supposed to do. This is one of those life situations in which a girl would be really helpful, but I didn't have one to talk to. Until that Sunday, when I wandered into the laundry room to fight again with the machine and spotted a teenage girl folding a pile of towels that was taller than she was. She was petite with tan brown skin, black hair and dark, sharp eyes. She looked familiar.

"You don't need to set it so high."

"What?"

"The machine. You don't need to set it so high. You'll ruin your T-shirts before their time. Set it to medium and you should be fine."

"Oh. Thanks."

"No problem."

I looked at her again, trying to place her face. I knew that I had seen those eyes somewhere. She also smelled like spices, a smell as exotic as her dark looks. She looked at me kindly with a soft smile on her face, and then I remembered; the day that I freaked out at George. The girl with the laundry basket in the hall.

"I'm Gordie."

"I'm Margarita."

I was about to make a joke, but she silenced me with her eyes. She knew exactly what kind of stupid thing that I was going to say.

"Yes, like the drink, and yes, I've heard all the old jokes, so don't even try one on me. I'm sure yours is not that original anyways."

"Hey, I'm a pretty smart guy. I can quip it up with just about anyone."

"Really?"

"Yeah. Some of the time. Not bad."

"Alright, go ahead and try one joke on me. But I warn you, I've heard plenty and if it fails to impress me, you won't get a second chance."

Dumb things flashed in my brain. Cinco de mayo jokes, lime in the coconut, dancing in the rain, whether or not she hooked up with daiquiri . . . . I had nothing.

She watched me with her hand on her hip, her eyebrow arched, waiting expectantly. She could see that I was struggling to find something smart to say and that I was failing. I shrugged.

"Ok, you got me. I'm not that smart."

"Maybe it's because your friend's not around to help you out? You sure had a lot to say to him."

"Yeah. Sorry you had to hear all that. I kind of lost it that day. I'm not usually that way."

"What's there to be sorry about? You spoke with a lot of passion. It's clear that you care for your friend."

"He's been going through a divorce. Rough times. He made the mistake of marrying an ice bitch and this is how it turned out."

"An ice bitch?"

"Sorry, excuse my language. You know, cold kind of person, really mean when they don't have to be?"

"No, no, I get it. It's just an interesting choice of words. Maybe you are sort of smart."

"Oh. Well, anyway, it's not the way I usually am and I just wanted you to know that. I'm a decent enough guy."

"Well, you stick by your friends. That's definitely a nice guy thing to do."

"Yeah. What else can you do?"

"Is he ok now?"

"I'm not sure. He's not talking much and I don't think that's a good thing. Trouble is, I'm not sure what to say to him myself. I've never been through this sort of thing before, since I've never been married. So I can't know what it's like to divorce."

"Understandable. I guess you can only be there for him."

"Yeah."

The machines were both going now. She kept folding towels, neatly and efficiently. The pile was growing on the table. It seemed like she was doing laundry for dozens of people. The only sound was that of the two machines, whirring away, angrily spinning clothes, with the thick smell of detergent in the air.

"Do you want a soda?"

"I'd like a Coke. Yes, please."

"Ok, be right back."

I went down the hall to the vending machine and bought a couple of Cokes and brought them back to the laundry room. She took the can of soda gratefully and sat down on the table, sipping and swinging her legs back and forth.

"You live here with your family?"

"Yes. My parents, my two sisters and my three bothers."

"Big family."

"We're Mexican," she shrugged, smiling as if that explained it.

"Oh."

"My family are immigrants. We moved here 10 years ago, but not all of us at the same time. It took a while to get us all here in Canada."

"Where from Mexico are you from?"

"Mexico City. The capital. Very big, polluted, crowded, dangerous. Not like here. Here, everything is so nice."

"Yeah. Your English is pretty good."

"We had a tutor. She was wonderful. A tall English woman named Jane. She did volunteer work in Mexico City and lived with us for 6 months. A very proper, serious lady. Are most ladies like that here?"

"Some. They're not always as friendly as you are."

"Ah. I figured as much. Papa says I'm too forward."

"Oh."

"He says that it will get me in trouble one day. Do you think he's right?"

"Maybe. You have to be careful. Guys have a way of misunderstanding things. They may think that you're inviting them or something."

"Inviting them to what?"

"How old are you?"

"Sixteen."

"Well, you have to be careful. That's all. People are more wary of strangers in North America. We're sort of brought up that way."

"Really? Are you brought up to be careful about everyone? I mean, you can usually tell a good person when you see one. Usually by looking into their eyes. A look will usually tell you when they're ok. Or a feeling."

"Yeah. People here don't trust their feelings as much, I guess."

"Hmm. No. I guess not."

"It's just one of those things that you have to get used to, I guess. It's not easy coming to a new place."

"Are you from here?"

"I was born and raised here. My parents were immigrants. They're from Europe."

"Ah. Do they like it here?"

"Yeah. They made a good life here. For themselves, for their kids. It's what everyone hopes for."

"It's true. My family as well. It hasn't been easy for us. My papa still drives taxis. He was a doctor back home. My mama cleans houses. She was an office clerk in the government back home. It's hard for them to find decent jobs. I guess it's because they still have thick accents. Mama especially. She has—how do you call it?—brokedown English?"

"Broken English. Yeah, it happens. She'll get better."

"I hope so. For all our sakes."

"Well, one day you will all find ways to provide for yourselves. When you're older, more educated, more integrated. Life will be good for you. It often is for the second generation."

"Is it so with you?"

"I guess. I have a good, steady job. I make a decent living, have a degree, that kind of thing. It's a pretty common story."

"That makes me hopeful."

"You have every reason to be hopeful. I'm sure you're a smart girl."

"I am a young woman."

"Sorry. Smart young woman."

"Don't you forget it, muchacho," she said, teasingly pointing her finger at me.

"What do you want to be, Margarita?"

"I want to be a career woman with a corner office. I want to be a mother with lots of beautiful children in a big house with my own maid and cook. And I want a handsome husband who's a loving father and gentle, kind person. And lots of expensive outfits."

"Ok . . ."

"What? Is it not a dream that all young women have?"

"Yeah, I think that's pretty accurate. But what do you want to do?"

"Work in business. Be my own boss. Make lots of money."

"Ok, fair enough. But do you know what business?"

"What does it matter what business it is? As long as it makes money. As long as it makes me happy."

"Are you counting on the money making you happy, or the business?"

"Aren't they one and the same?"

"Well, not if you don't like your business, no."

"Isn't all business more or less the same?"

"Not really. I mean, I work a job where I make decent money, but I hate it."

"You hate it?"

"Yeah. It's boring. It's stupid. Nothing really important gets done. I don't really feel like I contribute to society. But I definitely make money."

"That's so sad."

"It's not that bad, but it's no dream."

"Does the money make you happy?"

"The things that it pays for make me happy some of the time. It keeps me off the street. Is that good enough? I mean, I guess when you consider poverty, pollution and all the rest, yeah, it keeps me happy enough. But it's not happiness by itself, no."

"That's sad to hear. If it makes you so unhappy, why do you do it?"

"Well, nobody pays my bills for me."

"But if the money doesn't make you happy, shouldn't you do the thing that makes you happy and have less money?"

"It's not that easy when you get older."

"Why not? You have choices, you're an adult. I'm a teenager, I have no choices of my own. I have to go to school, I have to do chores . . ."

"You only have to do those things for another few years, and then you'll be an adult too. And being an adult isn't as easy as people say it is. You have your own choices to make, but you have responsibilities too, and you're alone to deal with them."

"I always thought that it would be easier as an adult, having your own place, your own space, going to work and coming home every night. I didn't think that it was going to be so hard as you're saying it is."

"I didn't think so either at your age."

"What did you think at my age?"

"I thought that it would be easier. I thought that it would be fun. That I would be free. I thought that a lot of things were possible that I just don't believe in now."

"Why don't you believe in them?"

"I guess because as I got older, I realized how much harder it is to get to your dreams, how much harder it is to break through into industries that are desirable, that there are a lot more obstacles than I would have imagined, some of them just plain weird. And real life takes money, and there's not a lot of money in dreams. Dreams take a lot of money."

"Hmm . . . . my mama often says that dreams are expensive."

"Sounds like my father."

"But my papa says that dreams are the only things worth having. Even if they are expensive."

"He sounds wise."

"He IS wise. You should come meet him. Come. We're making empanadas tonight. You can bring your friend too."

"Oh, I don't think that your parents are going to like you inviting us over like that without asking them . . ."

"Why not? We are neighbours. Neighbours help each other out, like I did with your laundry, and like you did by bringing me a Coke. We should make friends, no?"

"Oh, well . . . if you don't think they'll mind . . ."

"Of course not! I make lots of food. You can be my guests. I hardly ever have guests, father will be pleased. Come around 6. Everything should be hot by then. We're 505 at the end of the hall."

"Uh . . . I . . . . well . . . . ok."

"Good. Hasta luego, Hordie."

"See ya."

I had no idea what an empanada was, but I figured that it had to be good, so I piled up my laundry and headed back to the apartment to find Georgie. Georgie didn't want to go at first, but I convinced him that it would be good to know at least one person in the building other than me and we decided to go in the end. I figured that we should bring something, but all we had in the house was beer and cheese, so we brought a case of beer with us to the party.

It turns out that we made the right choice; the party was in full swing when we got there, a guaranteed noise complaint. Apartments 505, 506 and 507 were wide open and the party was spilling out into the hallway and onto the balconies. There was latin music, food, bottles of beer and cold fruity drinks, and big plates of the empanadas all around. The air smelled of spices, just like Margarita did, with the faint whiff of tequila and lemons. In the crowd of laughing people, I craned my neck looking for Margarita, feeling like I had landed in her native Mexico. Luckily, she found us.

Margarita smiled and came bouncing over in a light white linen dress. Her hair was pulled back in a high ponytail and she looked even younger than I had thought. She led us both into the apartment and introduced us.

"Everyone, this is Hordie and his friend-"

"Georgie."

"And his friend Hordie."

Everyone roared with laughter. When Margarita pronounced my name, she used a soft J-sound that came out like an H. When she said Georgie's name, she pretty much used the same sound. So it sounded like we both had the same name and they all thought that this was hilarious. We both looked at each for a minute, but then food and drink got shoved into our hands and we were being wheeled around the apartment, shaking hands and being kissed on the cheek by Margarita's sisters, and we both forgot to be shy or awkward.

One of Margarita's brothers grabbed me by the shoulders suddenly and led me around. It wasn't a rough gesture, but he was holding onto me pretty tight. He was a head shorter than me, but he had intense muscles and dark eyes that told me not to mess with him.

"This is la casa principale. It's where our parents live. Next door, is la casa de las hermanas. It's where the girls live. And the one next to it is the casa de los hermanos, where me and my brothers live. Nobody gets to the casa de las hermanas without passing by la casa de los hermanos. Nobody. Nadie. Comprende, muchacho?"

"Uh, yeah."

"So don't you and your friend there get any ideas about coming around when we're not here. Because one of us is always here. We protect our own, comprende? We are men of honour and so are our sisters, they are honourable too."

"Uh, yeah."

"Lay off, Jose, he's harmless. He's just a good neighbour."

"You—you be more careful when you invite people over. You can't trust just anyone who offers to buy you a soda."

"That's funny, that's what he told me too."

"Good man. I always tell my hermanas that they have to be careful with North American men, they don't understand things the same way. No offense, hombre."

"None taken. I told her the same thing."

"You see? You're two of a kind," she sighed, taking my hand. "Come. Papa wants to meet you now."

"I like you, hombre. But I'm watching you."

"Uh, yeah."

Jose tapped his eyes to show me that he was still watching, in case I didn't fully understand. I followed Margarita back into the apartment and she led me to the kitchen where her father was sitting at the table. All of the women were also there, making more mountains of empanadas. It seemed like they were never ending. I nodded at the women, but I honestly couldn't tell them apart. They all had the same beautiful skin, dark hair and eyes that Margarita had, and they seemed like visions floating around magically in the kitchen with big impossible plates of food.

Margarita's father was a character right out of the Mexican version of the Godfather. He was round, hunched, dark and his eyebrows looked sinister. He had black hair, a pencil thin moustache and drooping eyes like Marlon Brando. His voice was smoky and he had a heavy accent. I expected him to be more friendly-looking, considering the beauty of his daughters and Margarita's description of him.

I started to wonder if I should be worried as I approached. He looked capable of just about anything. But the dark exterior was a complete mask—he broke out into a huge smile when he saw me and poured tequila shots for us both and immediately began talking at a mile an hour.

"Come, come, Hordie, you need to have a shot of tequila with me, because a man can never truly know a man without having drank with him first, is it not true? And men who do not drink or who do not know how to drink are not the kind of men I trust. I do not like those men. They don't know how to enjoy life. They never inspire confidence in anyone and I have never in my life trusted or done business with a man who does not know how to enjoy life! Because that is really the biggest crime of all, is it not? An offense to God himself? To have life and not enjoy it? No, me, I believe that life has been created so that you can love it and live it to the fullest. It's what I have always believed and I don't think a man can live if he doesn't believe in something and I believe in that! There. Now, salud!"

He took the shot in one hefty swing and slammed it back down on the table. I did the same, mostly because it seemed impolite to not do the same, and he nodded his approval. He then poured two more shots.

"Now, Hordie, you are the first person that Margarita has brought to dinner and that's a good thing. I encourage my girls to meet people, even though they need to be careful who they talk to. But I trust my Margarita because she's such a smart young woman, even though she has the fiery temper like her mother, is it not so? Yes. But it seems like people in North America are too bland for her. She says that they have no fire, no spirit. It must be different for you, then? She obviously saw something in you. You must be interesting. You must have said something interesting at some point. And you must not be a dummy, right? Because she don't like no dummies either, she says they too dumb. And you must be kind, because she always say that North American men are not always kind in the way that they talk to each other. So tell me something about you, Hordie, what kind of man are you?"

"Uh, well, I'm just your average guy. You know, I work a stupid job, I come home, I have friends, I watch hockey, I drink beer. That kind of guy."

"Hockey? What is that, Hordie?"

"The sport. Hockey. I'm sure you've seen it, heard it, maybe on tv? The Ottawa Senators, you've heard of them?"

"Ah, yes, los Senatores. I have taken many borrachos to the game before in my taxi."

"You've taken burritos to the games?"

"No, no, borrachos. Drunken men."

"Oh, yeah, those."

"What makes people here love hockey so? It is not a beautiful game like our futbol."

"Well, maybe not to everyone, no. But hockey's a great sport. And it's really popular here in North America."

"So I see. But why? Explain this to me, hombre. I do not understand what is so great about it."

"Ah, well . . ."

We finished up our shots. He poured two more and looked at me, expectantly.

"Well, it's a part of our history, our heritage. Hockey is one of those games that brings the country together, because we're proud of it and we're proud of our players. It's a national pride, something that we identify with, even though we're all very different types of people. Most of us come from other countries, and we have our own traditions, but one thing that most of can share is hockey. It's a sport that demands a high level of skill and precision and speed. It not only celebrates our winters, it challenges it as well. It makes our winters seem less intimidating, like saying 'hey, we're not afraid of a little cold, we're not afraid of a little ice.' It's how the world looks from a frozen pond, how the ice sounds under the crush of skate blades, the slap of sticks, the energy of the other kids on the ice . . . it's that feeling that happens when you forget everything, forget the cold, forget all the problems in the world and you just feel . . . nothing. Nothing but happy."

"You really love it, don't you, hombre?"

"Yeah. I've loved it as long as I can remember. The first time that I ever saw a hockey game, I felt something inside me. It's in here. I can't explain it."

I pounded my chest to show him. He nodded, his eyes slightly glassy from alcohol, from emotion, I'm not sure which. I felt it too. The alcohol and the emotion, that is. He poured another set of shots for us and he looked at me with such fondness in his eyes and I couldn't remember the last time that someone looked at me that way and really looked at me. And really saw me for who I was, a person. Most of the people in my life seemed to look right past me, so disinterested in the things that I have to say as an average guy, a lowly bureaucrat and a dumb son full of dreams. But this man looked at me and he truly saw me, and didn't dismiss me as a nothing or a dreamer.

"To life, to you and to your love of hockey."

"And to you, sir."

"Salud!"

Wow, that tequila burned.

Chapter 23—Floating heads

I still wasn't in great shape by the time that Monday morning rolled around. I'm not sure what time I had rolled into bed, but the alarm went off way too early and neither Georgie nor I felt fit to drive in, so we both took a cab to work and couldn't face the thought of breakfast. I had lots of coffee on hand when Adventure Tim came in to see me.

"Hey, Gordie! How are you feeling? You look like shit, man."

"Yeah, I feel it. Was at a party last night, it was sort of a last minute thing."

"Yeah, those are always the best kind! You have the most fun when you don't plan shit."

"Yeah, that's true."

"Well, it's nice to see you having some fun for a change, man. You've been all serious and shit for a while now."

"Yeah, I know. This acting gig hasn't been the best thing for me."

"Well, at least you know for next time. Did you hear about Paul?"

"No. How's the mattress surfer doing anyway?"

"Not good, not good. He got caught."

"Caught?"

"Yeah, caught. With his pants down."

"What? How?"

"In the copy room with an intern."

"What is he, Bill Clinton?"

"His boss found them. Turns out that he was taking lots of coffee breaks and so was she. They thought that it was ok if it was all outside the office and stuff, since we can't tell anyone what to do when they're not here, but they were messing around right here."

"What? That's fucking nuts, man. What did they do to him?"

"Well, they can't hit him up with harassment because it was clearly consensual and she doesn't work for him, so they couldn't call it a violation in that way either. They got kind of stuck, you know, because he's a perm and they can't fire him for acting indecently because nobody really got harassed, so they had to put him on paid leave until they can figure out what to do with him."

"Wow. So he got caught acting lewdly in the office and they can't touch him?"

"Well, they can put a little note on his file, send him to gender sensitivity training, but no, there's not a heck of a lot that they can do to him. He might get suspended for a few weeks, but even that is hard to do. Once you get perm, it's hard to do anything to anyone. Man, I can't wait to get perm. Then it won't matter if I'm feeling up people in copy rooms, they'll just have to put me on leave as long as the girl wants to be felt."

"That is fucked up, man."

"Gordon. Your language. This is a place of business."

"Oh, yes, sorry."

It was my boss. It was time to head to another stupid meeting. I couldn't get over it. Don Juan Paul, messing around and getting caught and laughing it up at home on paid leave. This is why everyone hates the public service. They think that we go around and do stupid things and that we're untouchable. The employees with permanent status are pretty hard to fire, even when we do lunkhead things. Well, I guess this proves their point just fine. It made me wonder what it is that I could do to stay home and get paid. But that was just bad thinking, right there. I might not want to be in the office, but that didn't justify me doing stupid shit.

The stupid meeting was ready to start. I don't have any clue what it was about. I took my seat and chose a spot on the wall above the pot lights to look at when things got boring. I usually choose my spot early and need it early. The meeting began.

Sometime during this meeting, and I don't know precisely when, I had an out of body experience. Really. Not the weirdy beardy yoga transcendental meditation herbal tea kind of experience. I felt like I was entirely outside of my body, staring down at this strange board room full of floating heads that were talking but saying nothing. As they kept talking, I felt myself getting further and further away—almost like I was a non-being, dead somehow, yet still alive to witness this thing as if from a distance. It was completely odd.

And then it occurred to me that these people were the dead ones, not me. The floating heads, unreal, suspended in some alternate reality where nothing really mattered because they weren't really real. And then, in that moment, I felt real, I felt alive, more alive than any of them because the truth had struck me and had struck me so hard across the face that I couldn't deny that these floating heads didn't exist and I didn't have to listen to them anymore.

So I got up and left.

My boss came and yelled at me afterwards at my desk, telling me that I had made an embarrassment of him and he wanted to know how I had the gall to leave in the middle of an important meeting and what did I have to say for myself, and I could only stare back, thinking to myself: you're not real. This doesn't matter.

Afterwards, everyone would say that I was suffering the effects of the tequila from the night before, that it was just a bad hangover that clouded my judgement and made me incapable of understanding what I was doing at the time. But I knew that the real answer was not the after effects of the tequila, but the after effects of Margaritas' fathers' eyes and the way he truly saw me. I wanted to be seen and understood for a change, and floating heads weren't capable of that.

Chapter 24—A highly recommended vacation

From that moment on, all I saw were floating heads in the office. Except for Adventure Tim, who I actually knew and knew to be a real person, a thrill-seeking free sort of guy who loved everything that was supposed to be healthy. And Cheryl, the crying cubicle neighbour, who called up friends all of the time to tell them about her cheating ex-husband and how shitty it made her feel to be left for someone new, fresh, young and beautiful. Her tears took on a new meaning to me now; she was more than just an annoyance, she was a broken woman who had been replaced because she did the one thing that society doesn't permit women to do: age.

Her pain came to mean more to me than the meaningless long line of memos and reports and urgent emails. The management decided to have a meeting with me where they reprimanded me for 'my behaviour' and 'highly recommended' that I take a vacation. It was February and the hockey season was in full swing and the Senators looked better than ever, so I said yes. I resolved to get seats to the game, good ones, and take Margarita's father with me so that I could explain the fine details of the game to him. He has asked me to call him papa, which was weird because it wasn't weird. It felt natural to call him that even though he wasn't my father.

Before I left on my 'highly recommended vacation', I had flowers delivered to Cheryl with a simple note:

Forget the creep ex-husband and move on with your life. He doesn't deserve you. A friend.

She smiled for the first time in months.

I took Adventure Tim out for lunch at that weird organic vegan lunch counter that he likes and suffered through a tofu salad. Yes, a tofu salad, as if salad wasn't bad enough on its own without putting big chunks of tasteless soy in it. I guess it was healthy, because I left feeling like I hadn't eaten anything at all.

"So, how long you off for?"

"Two weeks. Should be enough to set me straight, or so they think."

"I can't believe it. Paul gets a paid leave for feeling up an intern in a copy room and you get 2 weeks vacation in the middle of February for walking out on a meeting. What a world."

"Yeah. Sorry about that."

"Well, not your fault. I'd do it myself if I could. But it's going to be shit boring in the office without you and Paul to talk to."

"You might have to make some new friends."

"Or date an intern."

"Keep me posted on your adventures, man."

"You make it sound like you're not coming back."

"I'm not sure about that. But it's going to be awhile before I see you again and I want to hear from you."

"No prob. Will keep you updated on the news, if anything actually happens."

"Thanks."

I went home and felt a lot better. Georgie was not, however. He was still acting moody and hadn't talked to me in days. It was clear that things still weren't resolved between him and Paula and that the divorce wasn't going smoothly. Whereas Roger had moved on and seemed like a new man with his girlfriend, Georgie wasn't making the transition well. I tried to coax him into coming to the pub to watch the game, but he just sat there on the couch holding his head in his hands. It didn't look good at all.

I'm not good at this shit, so I went down to see la casa de las hermanas. I knew it was odd to send over a girl that we barely knew to spend some time with Georgie to keep an eye on him, but I didn't know what else to do. Jose was in the hall in a flash, as if he had sensed a male presence outside his sisters' apartment.

"Are you looking for Margarita?"

"Yeah. I was hoping that she could talk to Georgie. He's having trouble and I don't know how to talk to him."

"What kind of trouble?" his eyes narrowed into little slits like a snake.

"He's going through a divorce. A rough one."

"Ah, yes, the one with the ice bitch, yes?"

"How did you know that?"

"Oh, we all know," he waved his hand. "He told us all about it over tequila. The poor man. He is in a bad way. We will talk to him. Margarita has homework—it's a weeknight. I will bring Consuela to talk to him. She is very good at these things."

"Thanks. I really appreciate it."

"No problem, hombre. We all need someone to talk to once in a while, and sometimes we need it to be a woman, they understand the things in the heart better than we do. I'll bring some tequila."

"Uh, thanks."

"You one of us, now, you now that, Hordie? We're like family, nothing is too much to ask."

"Oh. Oh. Ok."

"No problem. I get Consuela. We'll see you later."

"Yeah. Later."

I went to the pub to watch the game. Roger and his new girlfriend Sarah were there. Sarah was beautiful with long honey blonde hair and green eyes that would make me forget just about any ex in my life. She was fantastic and it was clear that she and Roger were a match. She got all his jokes and they sometimes seemed to be speaking their own private language. I never thought that I would see Roger looking so happy. He hadn't been that happy since . . . . his wedding day.

Stan the Man and Business Dan also brought girls with them. Stan had his sister with him, which didn't surprise me because he's the eternal bachelor and she's actually really cool. She used to be an alpine skier for Canada's Olympic Women's team until a fracture in her hip shortened her career. She was now a physiotherapist. Business Dan brought a work colleague who was clearly more than a work colleague; her name was Alice and she was an up and coming big shot in the same firm as Business Dan. She was competition for him, but also something else.

The game was fantastic. The pub atmosphere was also fantastic. We were crammed into that dining hall and everyone was watching the game intently. Even the servers stopped serving so that they could follow the action. You could feel the excitement, the tension in the room . . .

And when the final buzzer sounded and the Senators had won, we cheered and hugged each other like we had played the game ourselves. I hugged all of my friends at the table and felt better than I had in ages, happy to be with them, happy to see them happy, happy to just be . . .

And when I came home after midnight, there was Georgie fast asleep on the couch, with his arms around Consuela. She was beautiful like all of her sisters with same exotic features and gorgeous long black hair that trailed down to her waist. She had her arms wrapped around him and was stroking his hair. Jose was also asleep, with his arms around the lamp on the floor. There was an empty bottle of tequila on the coffee table and three shot glasses.

She put her fingers to her lips when she saw me and I nodded. I tiptoed my way to my bed and went promptly to sleep.

The next day, we all went out for breakfast together at the coffee shop around the corner. We didn't say much, but I could tell from the looks between him and Consuela that there was something happening, something good. When we got back to the apartment, we finally talked.

"So, how did it go?"

"Last night was really nice. Thanks."

"Did you get a chance to talk about what's going on?"

"Yeah. They listened to me, which was really good. I felt like they heard me, you know?"

"Yeah. I know."

"Things haven't been going really well. Paula's doing everything she can to delay the process and clean me out. She wants to keep the house, the car, and pretty much everything we own in the house, down to the last spoon. I'm trying to get her to be reasonable about things, but she refuses. I'm wondering if it would just be better to have the peace of mind, give her what she wants and just end it already."

"Well, it's not the worst idea. I mean, what is that shit really worth to you? Do you really care about the house, the car and all the stuff inside the house?"

"Not really. I just feel like she's still pushing me around. It's the principle, I guess. I put a lot in that house, too. Not just money, but labour, finishing the basement, painting, putting in new floors. And it's not the house itself. It's just the fact that she's calling the shots again and telling me that everything is hers. And it's not."

"Is it really worth fighting over? What if you just sell the house and split the profits and then you can both go your separate ways?"

"She doesn't want to do that; claims the house is her home."

"So be it. Doesn't she have to buy you out? Your half of the home's value?"

"Yeah, that's what my lawyer is arguing. And the lawyers. They're expensive and they don't care that she's delaying the process so much because it's putting money in their pockets. It aggravates me."

"You can't win with lawyers, I guess."

"No, you can't. But they're supposed to work for me. They're supposed to represent me. I just feel like nobody's on my side. My mom's giving me shit for failing in my marriage, and my lawyers don't give a crap about anything and can't do anything and there's Paula herself, in all her nastiness and bitchiness, just acting this way to drive me crazy. This isn't what I wanted. I wanted to be settled, normal, happy. I never planned on getting divorced and having my life turn to shit like this."

"Well, nobody ever plans to have shit happen to them but it does."

"I'm a loser, Gordie."

"Oh, fuck no, Georgie. You're not a loser. Shit happens to everyone. We all try our best and we sometimes fall on our asses, but you're not a loser. You're leaving a shitty relationship. It doesn't matter what happened in it, that's the past. You know it's shitty and that's why you're leaving. That's a good thing. You have any idea how many morons would just hang around because it's easier? Because they don't want to bother having to cook their own meals and learn to do laundry? You're better than that shit, Georgie, you're taking a stand and you're going to be happier for it one day. I promise."

He had his face tucked in his hands while he sat on the couch, but I knew that he had heard me. Man, I hope he wasn't crying.

"You're right, man. Maybe not today, maybe not tomorrow, but I'll feel better someday."

"That day may be sooner than you think if Consuela keeps coming around . . ."

"Shut up!"

His smile told me that I was right.

Two days later, we got prime seats in the 100 level for the Sens game on the Centre ice line. I got seats for Georgie, Consuela, Margarita, Jose, myself and Papa. We took a cab with one of Papa's friends so that none of us would have to drive home. I made sure that we got there early so that we could settle into our seats and enjoy all the pre-game fanfare, like the marching band and the warm up skate. I was eager to explain the finer points of the game to Papa and he was eager to learn. We went to our seats loaded down with jumbo hot dogs, popcorn, and beer—Margarita had a Coke.

"So what are they doing now on the ice? What's that machine?"

"That's the Zamboni. It clears the ice and makes it nice and smooth, so that when the players get on it, it's fresh for them. A fresh sheet of ice makes it easier to skate."

"Ah, yes, of course. Now who are those?"

"Those are the linesmen and the referees. They make sure that the rules are followed, just like in futbol."

"There are so many of them."

"There are a lot of rules in hockey."

"I see."

Papa got a quick understanding for the game, and for its many rules, as I explained every penalty, every power play strategy, every little nuance that came to mind during the course of the game. I showed him which of the players were the best on the team, what the stats meant in the game booklet and by the time that the game ended with a victory, he was chanting Alfie with the rest of the crowd and whipping a towel over his head.

Georgie and Consuela looked lost in a world that was their own. I don't even think Georgie remembered that we were at a game. Jose and Margarita chatted during the game as well, but mostly munched happily on popcorn, just happy to be there. But Papa really got into it, his cheeks rosy and shiny from beer and crowd enthusiasm. He really liked it.

"When can we come back again?" he asked me on the way home.

"There's another home game next week. We can go then."

"Good, good. Just you and me next time, Hordie. The rest can carry on with other things. I need you to tell me more about this Spezza person—why does he drop the puck to nobody?"

"We've been trying to figure that one out for a long time now."

"What is he trying to do there?"

"He's trying to sneak off the puck to someone else without the opposition figuring it out. Sometimes it works and when it does, it's beautiful. But when it doesn't, well, it just looks shit stupid."

"Ah, like when you do something to impress a girl and you fall on your face?"

"Yeah, exactly like that. No guts, no glory, that kind of thing."

"No guts, no glory? Hmm. Crude. But I like it."

"Yeah, it works."

"I don't know if I like it as much as I like futbol. I don't love it yet. But there's something to this and I like it so far. I want to see more of this hockey."

"Sure."

"It's good that you love it, Hordie. It's good that you have something to love in your life."

"Well, it's not exactly like having a woman, but yeah, it's a good kind of love."

"Women is better. But they can be trouble. But better to love something than nothing, right?"

"Yeah, I guess."

We stumbled home that night, happy, stuffed and maybe slightly drunk. It was the way that I often felt with the family. Papa and I did get seats to the next game and it was fun to see him get into it—he even called an icing, which surprised the hell out of me, and yelled at Spezza. We had some pretty good seats, although I doubt Spezza heard, but it was hilarious to watch him turn indignant and start yelling at him in Spanish. Yes, in Spanish. Only in Canada would you find that many fans yelling in just about every language around the world at their hockey players.

"Our team is winning, Hordie. How long do you think that they can keep winning?"

"Papa. You said our team."

"Did I? I guess I did. Yes."

"That's great."

"Yes. How long do you think our team will keep winning?"

"I don't know. I hope that they can keep it up a long time. They may take a run at the Cup."

"What is the Cup?"

"The Stanley Cup. The Holy Grail of Hockey—the one and only big prize. The hardest trophy to win in professional sports. You need to win 82 regular season games just to compete for it! Then you need another 16 games to get it. You need to be in the top teams and then fight your way through 4 rounds, including a Conference final. But it's the biggest prize there is and once you get your hands on it, your whole life changes. You become the champion of champions. It says that you're the best in the world. There's a parade in your city after it happens, the players drink champagne out of it, and everyone gets to spend a day with the Cup afterwards in their home town so that everyone can applaud them."

"Wow. It's what you call a big deal?"

"It's a pretty big deal, papa."

"Do you think it could happen here?"

"Maybe. They're having a great season, who knows? It would really be something if that happened. It might inject some life into this town."

"Who knows?"

It could. It could happen here one day. The thought carried me through until the end of February. Until I had to go back to work.

Chapter 25—Chasing Stanley

Work didn't matter. Divorces didn't matter. Family didn't matter. The only thing that mattered was the Chase for the Cup.

The month of March passed by in a blur of hockey games. While things charged on at work and more boring meetings were called, the Chase for the Cup continued, fast and furious. You couldn't find a single seat in the pub on game nights and we screamed ourselves hoarse until the last buzzer. La casa de las hermanas decided to feed us idiots during the run and showed up at our door with big platters of tortillas, the real kind. It was like a sneak preview of what heaven looks like.

I went into work like a robot and punched out promptly at 5pm. My 3 months probation was up on the job, so they couldn't just drop me whenever they wanted to, although it was pretty clear that they wanted to. My boss seriously regretted promoting me to the high heels job, but pulling me at this point was only going to injure his reputation, like the coach who starts the wrong goaltender for the big game, but can't change him without losing face. It was a war of attrition within my office, and it wasn't clear who was winning. One thing that I knew for sure was I wasn't going to sit around in an office while the Sens won the Cup—I was going to be in the crowds, in the bars, in the stands, screaming my fool head off.

So I might have been committing career suicide. So be it. I never considered my job to be a career; the prospect depressed me too much. It would have been impossible to get out of bed in the morning without believing in some back part of my mind that I wasn't always going to do this job. That's the kind of hope that I needed to not push thumb tacks into my eyes.

La casa de los hermanos wanted to get on board too. They showed up at our door just about every night with a bucket full of beer on ice and a bottle of tequila. I had no idea where they got all that tequila; it seemed like a never-ending supply, like the big impossible plates of food delivered by the beauties from la casa de las hermanas. Consuela was around more often than anyone else. It was really time to move on that divorce.

Those were noisy, boozy, unforgettable nights. While the weather outside got sloshy and grey and the city looked even uglier under murky skies, we spent our nights either in warm, friendly pubs that were full to capacity, surrounded by big screens and the game in perfect HD, or we were at home on the couch, surrounded by friends and platters of delicious food. I spent a lot of time explaining the game to los hermanos and Papa and it reignited my love for it. I hated all of the time that I had wasted doing senseless work. I loved coming home at night—everything was so exciting, so fresh, so animated.

April couldn't come fast enough. Not just because the weather got better, not just because the end of the fiscal year in government meant that we could all finally breathe for a while; but because the Stanley Cup Finals were set to begin and we were a part of it.

The overtime that I had put in at work was paying off; I managed to score tickets to the playoffs with almost no problem at all. I didn't get the best seats; we were back up in the bleachers, but that's where the real fans sit. That's where it's the loudest, proudest and where the most booing happens. So I was right where I wanted to be. Plus, I loved having the full panoramic view of the ice so I could see how things would play out. I would draw diagrams on napkins for Papa and he thought they were delightful. And the whole building shook.

It was the stuff that dreams are made of. I jumped at every missed puck, I shouted at every bad call, I cheered with every goal, and I booed everything that moved from the opposite side. Every team became the enemy—there was no time for swing teams or shared allegiances. I couldn't cheer on the Habs. I couldn't watch any other Canadian team other than my own. It was time to live and die by the Senators.

The Sens played their first round of the playoffs against a shaky, inexperienced Pittsburgh team. Despite the fact that they had the team's hottest prospect in Sidney Crosby, the first round was a rough lesson for the kid from Cole Harbour. They gave the young star no time or space on the ice at all and swerved around him like dervishes. They went down in 5 games in what hardly even looked like a fight.

Then it was on to New Jersey and I had visions of goaltender Marty Brodeur crushing everything that came towards him and all of our dreams with it. A lot of people expected that this would be their swift exit from the playoffs, but they were wrong. New Jersey's big names couldn't make enough smooth moves against Ottawa's top line or top shot blocker Anton Volchenkov and they also went down in 5 games. The momentum had swung heavily in Ottawa's favour now. A third round of the playoffs almost seemed too good to be true, but there was another large hurdle left: the Buffalo Sabres and Ryan Miller.

The Sabres and the Senators are pretty common foes with a good history of animosity. They've been known to mix it up and it was strangely satisfying to know that this was Ottawa's chance to get Buffalo kicked out. It was going to take sheer firepower to take out Buffalo who couldn't score worth a damn, but had one of the best goaltenders to walk the earth. There was good reason to fear. Emery was nowhere near the level of Miller, trying to make up for in attitude what he didn't have in talent and not coming anywhere close to either.

It was an intense but short series. And short tempered. The fights between the benches were almost as intense as the battles on the ice. I'll never forget how Lindy Ruff looked that night, how it seemed that his head might actually pop off his neck from pressure as he yelled a blue streak and how Bryan Murray matched him word for word. Murray, who's usually fairly reserved and doesn't do much more than wave his hand in frustration. He was definitely feeling the pressure.

Incredibly, this series was also won in 5 games with a miracle of a shot from Alfredsson through 3 players and into the net. Ottawa had fought its way through Pittsburgh, New Jersey and division rivals Buffalo to make its way to the Cup Final. The paper ran a series on how the last time that Ottawa had won the Cup was in 1927. It had been 80 years and the old Senators had been playing in the Civic Centre downtown at Lansdowne Park. The old pictures from that period splashed out on the front page made us nostalgic—and hungry.

The Senators were a great team that year—but they also had great leadership. Alfie's pictures were on every sports page and every sports network was talking him up. Not that we could blame them.

"I love this Alfredsson—he looks just like a Swedish Viking, no? He has such quiet strength and determined eyes. Look at his eyes."

We all looked at Alfredsson's eyes and we had to agree with Papa.

"He's a Viking King. A King of Kings."

"A God among men. A hockey God."

"A golden warrior."

"A fearless leader."

"Like Zapato."

We all stared at Jose. He shrugged.

"You know, a leader."

"Ah."

"What about this Chris Neil? Why does he fight all the time? He's not a big man."

"Well, you know, he's an enforcer. He likes to get at people."

"Shouldn't they have someone at least twice his size? Why doesn't someone else do it?"

"They're not really a rough team."

"Does that mean that they don't fight?"

"It means that they don't really play a very physical game."

"Oh. Is that going to be bad for them later on?"

"It might be. Depends on whether or not they can change up their game enough to beat the opposition. It looks like it's going to be the Anaheim Ducks."

"Anaheim?"

"Yeah."

"What does Anaheim have that Ottawa doesn't have?"

"A dirty team."

"What is a dirty team?"

"Well, they're not known to be the most honest men in the league."

"They play without honour. Very bad. They don't deserve to win if they play without honour."

"I agree."

"It is my hope that these men without honour do not win."

"Mine too."

The feeling was contagious. Hockey fever swept the nation. It felt like something monumental, like being part of a revolution, except that we weren't actually doing anything. We just felt so together. The whole city seemed to take on a new life. Banners were popping up all over the place and Elgin street turned into Sens Mile, teeming with people in red, out in support of their team. It finally felt like 'our' team. Gone were the fair-weather fans. They were replaced by the diehards. They were full of face paint and pride. And in the midst of it all was our great God Daniel Alfredsson.

I started dreaming about the glory of a Stanley Cup Parade down Elgin Street, winding its way to Parliament Hill where the leaders of the country could bless it and make some stupid speech that we would actually cheer for. I imagined Alfredsson heading that parade in the lead car like Miss America, waving to the crowds, cradling the Cup in his arms, the sun shining off its steely frame. Spezza and Heatley would also be there, smiling like school kids, Spezza with that goofy laugh and Heatley with that gap-toothed smile. And Ray Emery would be partying like a gangster, surrounded by hot women in a Ferrari or something ridiculous like that, chugging $250 bottles of champagne. And in the background would be Queen singing *We Are the Champions* on a continuous loop . . .

That was the year that Alfie could do no wrong. He could have run for Prime Minister and we would have all showed up to vote in droves. We loved the man. Every red blooded hockey fan had a man crush on Alfie. We wanted to be him. Signs showed up in the streets with "In Alfie, We Trust." It couldn't have been more true.

Even Papa got in the spirit of it all and named a burger after Alfie. It didn't actually have anything at all to do with him, but it did have yellow mustard on it to show his Viking roots. Actually, nobody really got it except for Papa who invented it, but he made them every night the Senators played in that Cup Run. He was incredibly superstitious in his beliefs, and like most sports fans, believed that certain rituals were going to help guide our team to victory. So every game night, he would make the Alfie burger and we would get together in my living room to watch the game as a family, with los hermanos and Consuela present.

Nobody was allowed to miss the game, not even Georgie, who should have been at more legal battles with Paula. But the beautiful thing about it? He was standing her up. He was leaving her and her expensive lawyers in the dust, waiting for him while the clock ticked and the hours racked up more money, and he said fuck it all and came home religiously to watch the game with us every night. I'm sure Consuela had something to do with that.

Sens gear was disappearing fast, but I managed to call around and get my hands on Alfredsson T-shirts for myself and all the hockey loving family in time for the Final round against the Ducks. Yes, it was finally here. The big Final against the mean, nasty, ugly brutes of Anaheim. The men without honour.

On the night of game one, I presented the T-shirts. Everyone received them with big smiles and immediately put them on. It was funny how we all matched and of course Consuela had to take our picture. We were all swimming in them because they were X-large. I'm surprised that we weren't all X-large after the plates of food and beer we packed away during the season leading up the Final.

"So, in keeping with playoffs tradition, none of us are allowed to wash the T-shirts until the series is done and won. Nobody is allowed to mention the name Stanley, because if you say it too soon, it might not happen. And finally, nobody is allowed to shave from this moment on."

"No shaving?," asked Consuela.

"No. We have to grow the playoff beard. It's how we show solidarity for our team."

"It doesn't sound very nice."

"It isn't very nice."

"You must not question tradition," scolded Papa. "And now, I have a tradition too that must be followed."

There was a knock on the door. Papa nodded at Jose and he went to open it. Georgie and I looked at each other, since neither one of us had invited anyone else tonight. We both shrugged and then turned around.

"Jesus!"

Wrong thing to say. We both looked down at our hands, apologetic. There was a priest at the door and he looked none too pleased to see us. But he looked happy to see Papa.

"Boys, this is Padre Alvarez. He's the priest who blessed our home when first we arrived in Canada and he has been our spiritual father ever since. Tonight, he has come to bless this series, this team and pray to guide us to victory in the quest for the Cup."

He was serious. A Catholic Priest had showed up to my door in order to bless the Final Round of the 2007 Stanley Cup series and pray God that the Ottawa Senators would be victorious. It was one of the oddest moments of my life.

I know that I've often thought that hockey was a religion in my life, but this was one step further than even I had thought.

But there it was. We were asked to form a circle around the priest and hold hands. We all bowed our heads while the Priest laid down the blessing and then sprinkled us with Holy Water. Yes, holy water. When it was all over, he walked around to each of us with the cross and asked us to kiss it. I didn't want to be rude, so I obliged. I think that I had offended him earlier when I had yelled Jesus at the sight of him, so I suppose that helped to make it up.

The blessing went like this:

"Oh, Heavenly Father, we ask you today that you help guide our team—The Ottawa Senatores—to victory in the Stanley Cup Finals against the Men without Honour—the Anaheim Ducks. Help them to play with strength, heart and honour, so that they may inspire others to greatness with their sense of decency and fair play and let them not be injured in their quest for victory, but let them persevere and bring great joy to the city. Amen."

That's really what he said. I could not have made that up.

Then out came the plates of Alfie burgers and beer and we were ready for puck drop.

The dirty Ducks had home ice advantage, so the first game was played in Anaheim at the Honda Centre. I told the guys to keep an eye out for Chris Pronger—he had a bad reputation around the league for dirty acts and he was big, mean and ugly. Papa and los hermanos actually jeered loudly every time that we saw him on the ice. I also told them to keep an eye on Anaheim's Captain, Scott Niedermayer, not because he was dirty, but because he was good. We knew that it wasn't going to be an easy series and a quick look across the Anaheim bench was a good indication that it was going to be a bruiser. There was a joke going around that this series was Beauty vs the Beast—with a good looking Ottawa team going against a brutish looking Anaheim goon squad.

California Governor Arnold Shwarzennegger, aka, the Governator, showed up for the ceremonial puck drop. After the Catholic blessing, it was the second weirdest thing that I had seen that night. There were big question marks hanging over the entire series. It was rare to see sunshine state teams in the Finals, so there were questions surrounding the quality of the ice. It was also rare to see the Sens go head to head with the Ducks, a team that they had almost no history with. History was about to be made between the two teams now.

The things that worried me the most in this series was the reputation of the Ducks for making dirty plays and getting away with them and J.S. Giguere's quality goaltending compared with Emery. Emery was doing the job alright, but he had a tight defense core in front of him to help him out. Emery had a bad habit of being a bit of a hothead and I wasn't convinced of his technical skills—the guy just seemed more flash and dash to me. The advantage in net was definitely there for Anaheim.

Then there was the scrapping. There wasn't a lot of scrapping leading up to the Final because they don't play a highly physical game in the Eastern Conference. Buffalo had pretty much relied solely on Ryan Miller to push them through and that hadn't worked for them. Pittsburgh looked awkward and disorganized in their series and the boring style of the New Jersey Devils did them in leading up to this moment. But nobody had really laid down the boom on the Senators on their Cup Run; they were a dynamic, fast-paced team that liked to score off their main line and when given enough time and space, they ran over the teams in the East. But the West was different and a lot harder to win.

My worst fears came true in the first 2 games of the series, as Anaheim charged to a commanding 2-0 lead in the series at home, taking both games by one point. They won game one by a score of 3-2 and game two by a score of 1-0, an embarrassing shutout where the magic line of Alfredsson, Heatley and Spezza failed to capitalize. The Sens were putting on a good show, but they were being outplayed and took some boneheaded penalties. It was time for the tide to change in Ottawa.

When the series made its way into town, we were ready. Papa and I went to the game together and sat up in the 300 level in probably the last two seats available ever since the Cup Run began. When it looked like the Sens might make it, I reserved my seats in advance and I was so glad that I had. Everyone complained bitterly that I wasn't taking them; it was a funny time to be a fan. Even people who couldn't have cared less about hockey and didn't know what an icing was, actually cried bitterly about the fact that I didn't take them to the game instead.

But I couldn't wait. I wanted to go to this game since I was a kid. I had dreamed about this kind of thing happening here. All across the country, people were claiming Ottawa as Canada's team and were throwing their support behind them, even people across the prairies and in the Maritimes. It was just wild. We got to Scotiabank Place 3 hours before the game was set to start and there was already a crowd forming. Kids were getting their faces painted, promoters had set up beer tents and replica Cups with tinfoil on them, and there was a live band playing. It was a festive air and a fresh spring breeze underlined the general feeling of wellbeing.

We picked up beer, hot dogs and popcorn before heading to our seats to watch the warm up. It was already crazy loud in the building and nothing had happened yet. There were towels slung over the seats for us to whip. The big joke in town was that tonight's special was duck. The crowd had trouble quieting down for the anthem, but we respectfully stood for both anthems. When they had finished and were lining up at centre ice for the faceoff, I looked over at Papa and he was hunched over in his seat, his head on his hands that were locked together in prayer. He was praying for victory and it suddenly didn't seem so crazy.

I remember every feeling of that game. Not every play, not every second, not every line change. I remember every feeling—the ecstasy when the Sens scored their 5 glorious goals, the disgust and outrage when Pronger hit McAmmond, the way that the whole building seemed to hold its breath when a shot missed the net. Every pass seemed to happen in slow motion. Every blow felt like my own ribs were crushed to the boards. I could feel the cold air on my face as the players whipped up the ice, each bristle of my playoff beard on edge. The feeling was electric; we were finally united, we were finally one. And our team came through.

"Oh, Hordie, Hordie, I don't believe it! We won! We won!"

Papa looked at me with shining eyes. Even I almost felt like crying—crying with joy. We hugged each other and then started hugging just about everyone around us. It took us three hours to get out of Scotiabank Place and downtown, and everywhere there were cars honking all along the highway. People were hanging out their windows yelling in joy. Elgin Street was already crowded by the time that we got there with drunken revellers singing and chanting. Already we could see the parade route down Elgin street leading up to Parliament Hill where a great speech would be made and Alfredsson would hoist the Cup over his head and smile.

But it all came crashing down in the pivotal game 4 and the incident that would make Alfredsson's name mud in California for the rest of his life. In the dying seconds of the second period, Alfredsson chucked the puck at Ducks Captain Scott Niedermayer, resulting in general outrage on the ice. It was a horrible moment. We couldn't even look at each other. We all wanted to believe that it was an accident, like he said later on. But it only looked one way to Anaheim and they muscled their way to a 3-2 victory in game 4. It was a turning point in the series and Papa looked at me mournfully, shaking his head.

"He has lost his honour. The series is lost."

I refused to believe it, but it was true. Game 5 was a do-or-die situation and we died. Our collective season-long dream of a Stanley Cup parade led by Alfredsson died on the stick of Travis Moen as he clinched the win. To this day, I can't stand Travis Moen for having killed our dream. The defeat was utterly crushing. To lose to the Ducks, a California team. To not reclaim the Cup after 80 years—yes, 80 whole years—without one. It was the saddest moment.

The city went quiet. Elgin street was abandoned, like a post-zombie apocalypse city. The fans turned back into their normal, cynical, non-loyal selves, some of them claiming that they had never believed that it would happen in the first place, and others, claiming that they knew that we couldn't possibly outplay the Ducks. The Faithful maintained that the series was bought by Bettmann to increase interest in the NHL in the state of California, which had been blessed with 3 NHL teams, while there were others who simply stated that the Ducks had cheated their way to the Cup. You could feel the bitterness, disappointment and general sour feelings all across the city as people abandoned the team and their dreams and went back to their summertime habit of invading patios downtown and complaining about life.

Myself included. Life looked pretty bleak without the Cup to hope for. Despite the return of warm weather, I didn't feel like celebrating. The wounds were deep and I just wanted to hide somewhere and lick them. Papa said we all needed some quiet time alone to reflect, which was good for us and for our livers.

It wasn't all bad news. Georgie's divorce was finalized and his lawyers had finally convinced the Ice Bitch to settle. As a result, Consuela was around all of the time and both of them were looking pretty happy. But I had more free time to think about all of the things in my life that I didn't like and it was something that I didn't want.

The rest of the month was just work and pubs, but it didn't feel the same anymore. There were no games to watch and the spirit had been sucked out of the bars and instead of being welcoming, they were just bars. Bars that could be anywhere, bars that meant nothing, places that did business. They were interchangeable and I didn't care where we went anymore or what we did. I was in a post-Cup run depression, but worse, I was back to my old life. My meaningless, stupid life.

Chapter 26—Go for the Gusto

People noticed. My friends were sort of worried about me in their own quiet way without saying it. Margarita noted that I was often in moods. And Papa decided to have a heart to heart with me one Friday night over another bottle of tequila.

"Why you so unhappy, Hordie? I know it's not just the hockey."

"I've always been this unhappy, Papa. Only hockey makes me that happy. I work a stupid job for stupid people. I have nobody in my life. My family thinks that I'm a loser. I hate this stupid city. This is just the way it's always been, but hockey lets me forget all that and now, that's not possible anymore."

"If you feel that way, what keeps you going? Why do you even wake up in the mornings?"

"I guess because there's always going to be another season, another hope, another dream."

"But that's not good enough for a man to live on. Nobody lives vicariously through something else. What do you have, Hordie? What do you have for you, what are you proud of?"

"Nothing, Papa. I'm proud of nothing I've done because I've done nothing."

"I don't believe that."

"Well, it's true. I'm knucklehead. A dreamer. And you can't have dreams when you don't have money."

"Now that's enough! That's enough! That's bad talk! Dreams keep us alive! Dreams are all we really have! And it doesn't take money; any idiot can make money. Any idiot can find money wherever he wants, he can find it in the street if he wants, he can win it off a scratch card! It doesn't take money to get what you want—it takes guts. Guts! What is your saying again? No guts, no glory. That's exactly it! You can't do anything unless you go out and do it and that takes guts!

You need to make a decision—a real one—a decision that's right for you even if people think you're a fool! It's better to be a fool with dreams, it's better to be a fool who tries, than a fool who has none and has never tried and has nothing to show for his life! How can you think this way, Hordie? You love something. You know you love something, you feel it inside. Remember how you said you felt, the first time that you saw hockey? Remember how you felt something inside? How it touched you? That's real, that's something. Not this life where you hate your job and your city. Not this life where you feel bad about yourself because you don't have what everyone else has, what everyone else thinks you should have.

You know how a person finds happiness in this world, Hordie? It's not in the arms of woman, it's not in a bottle of tequila, it's not in your bank account. We find happiness in the world when we have something to love. And it doesn't matter what that something is, as long as we're true to it and do something with it. You have love in your system—do something with it!"

"But Papa, it's not that easy. I can't play, I don't have any experience . . ."

"That's nonsense! Listen, I have many children and if ever I see them as unhappy as you are, I die. I die inside. I can't stand to see that kind of suffering, not when you're young and free and can do anything you want with your life! You just stopped believing in it and you just stopped believing in yourself. That's criminal! To be young like you, to be free, to be a man, to be one's own man and not have the cajones to shape your life into something you love! How can you be so blind? How can you let yourself turn into a bitter shell of a man? Because that's what you will be if you keep this up. You need to make a change, Hordie, you need to do it. For you."

"I can't live off love, Papa. I need to pay bills. My job pays bills . . ."

"And it makes you feel worthless. That's not worth paying any bill."

"What am I supposed to do, just call up the NHL and ask them to hire me? Hey, I'm Gordie, a hockey nut, but I only play armchair hockey because I'm a fan and you wouldn't by any chance have a job opening for a loser like me with no experience doing anything interesting?"

"Maybe leave out the word 'loser'."

"You are kidding me . . ."

"I am serious. I never kid when someone's happiness is at stake. I'm Catholic."

He folded his hands in front of him as if that was settled. I started trying to make sense of that sentence, but it didn't quite work. I took the shot of tequila in front of me. Papa poured off two more and kept a serious look on his face the whole time, like when the priest had come to my place to bless the series.

It was a ridiculous thought. But was it really that ridiculous? I mean, a lot of people worked in the NHL, did they not? They didn't have the glamourous jobs like broadcasting, but they needed people to sell tickets, do merchandising, marketing, finance. They were a business like any other business and they had the same needs. I wasn't a person in business, but I had enough experience working in an office setting to do some of the stuff that they needed. As we sat there and talked it over, it seemed less and less like a stupid idea, as often happens when you're drinking tequila together.

Considering my options again with a clear head on Monday morning, I began to cruise the NHL site for jobs. And strangely enough, there were more of them than I thought, mostly in sales and mostly in sunshine states, where hockey wasn't the big draw that it was in Canada. There was a demand for people who could talk hockey at a competent level and encourage sales. Could I be that kind of person?

"Gordon, my office, two minutes."

My boss. Crap.

Adventure Tim leaned over his cubicle wall and shook his head at me. This was a sure sign that trouble was headed my way. I went over to him. He looked serious for a change.

"Today's not a good day for him, man. You're probably going to get it bad. If you're going to get in trouble, today would be the day to go for the gusto."

"What?"

"Go for the gusto. Do a good one. It may as well be worthwhile."

"What are you talking about?"

"I'm just saying that this isn't a day for little trouble. It's a day for big trouble, so go ahead and let the stupid cock know what you think of him."

"Are you crazy? You're telling me on the day that my boss is pissed off and ready to blow a gasket, that I should use today to tell him off?"

"Why not? As good a day as any other," he shrugged. "Anyway, he's so worked up, he probably won't even notice."

"I sometimes don't get you, Tim. If I didn't know you any better, I'd think you wanted to sabotage me and take over my job."

"Yeah, your job is so worth taking."

"True, but that doesn't mean it's worth losing like that."

"I say go big or go home. In any case, he's going to rip into you about your job performance. I say don't take that shit lying down."

"My job performance?"

"Yeah, it's time for your annual review and a lot of people have noticed your negativity. It stinks, man, and they're going to nail you for it. That's what you're going in for."

"Shit."

"Yeah. Good luck."

"Yeah."

I made my way to my boss' office and closed the door. He was sitting behind his desk with his hands folded in front of him, as if he was about to lecture the dog for bringing mud into the house. He motioned with his head that I should sit. I took the chair facing him and waited for him to speak. He looked at me for a long minute in silence and then shook his head slowly, as if he was talking to himself. He then took off his glasses and began to polish them.

This must be his psychological tactic. Make me wait in silence and then tend to other things like I'm not even in the room. He had called me in here and he wanted to make it clear where the power lay. I just sat there and waited for him to say something. I hated this.

When he had finally finished the glasses to his satisfaction, he put them on his face and adjusted them accordingly, as if he had noticed me for the first time. He then set his gaze directly upon me and folded his arms together, leaning towards me like Larry King Live.

"I have to talk to you today, Gordon, about something that has been brought to my attention and to the attention of others. I have to say that I'm not happy about this talk, but it has to be done. I need to talk to you, as your manager, about your attitude."

"My attitude, sir?"

"Yes, your attitude. It has been painfully obvious that you are in a negative mind frame most of the time. It does not appear that you enjoy your job or that you appreciate the new opportunities that have been afforded to you within this organization. As well, your blatant disrespectful actions, walking out of meetings for example, have been a cause for concern and my own superiors have questioned my decision to promote you to your current acting position. I myself, frankly, have also questioned that decision in light of your recent actions and it pains me that your behaviour is negatively reflected on me as well. As your manager, I am responsible for ensuring that employees act in a courteous and professional manner and to my mind, you have not done so."

I waited for him to go on. He looked at me expectantly, as if I was going to defend myself or apologize. I honestly couldn't think of anything to say. The part of my brain that remembered the tequila conversation wanted to spit in his face and tell him that if the job hadn't been made for monkeys, I would have enjoyed it more. The part of my brain that was in control was not Gordie, though. It was Gordon, who just stared back.

"How do you feel about your behaviour this year?"

"Nothing, sir."

"Nothing? You feel nothing about your negative behaviour and its effect on people around you and the fact that you've made me look bad?"

"I feel nothing, sir, because this job means nothing to me. It pays the bills, but as far as I'm concerned, a job at Blockbuster would be the same."

"Is that so?"

He arched an eyebrow at me and then unfolded his hands. For a minute, he leaned back in his chair, and then, he got up and began to pace the room. He folded his hands behind his back like an army general in a movie. I'm sure he had such grand thoughts about himself.

"I'm highly disappointed in you, Gordon, not only because of the poor performance that you put in this year, and for the poor performance report that I will have to submit regarding you this year, but also, because of your lack of respect and dedication for your career. A career in the public service is a respectable one. A career in the public service means that you dedicate your life to helping Canadians and aiding the government in providing for the people. Many of us are privileged to play the roles that we do in society, to give of ourselves in the service of others. We make the country run; we are its life blood. And the fact that you don't take any pride in that is a disappointment all around."

"No offense, sir, but I don't see it that way. I don't think we do much more than push the papers around. In fact, I'm convinced that a highly talented monkey could do what I do, pushing buttons, shuffling through email, correcting typos on reports that don't go anywhere . . . you may think that we provide essential services to the people, but we are so far away from the people. We don't work on the ground. We don't visit their homes. We don't experience their lives as they do or see their pain. In fact, I feel even less connected to the people when I'm here in this office tower surrounded by papers. Nothing I do brings them food or water or brings them any closer to social equality. I don't even bring a smile to their faces. I think that the people down at the coffee shop appreciate me more than the people; at least, I make them smile."

He was clearly taken aback. He stopped shuffling around the office and planted himself back into his chair so that he could face me and his face looked grim.

"It's not all about smiles, Gordon. We have to do the things behind the scenes to make things happen in life, the so-called boring stuff."

"I know that someone has to do it, but I don't think that someone has to be me."

"What are you saying, then, Gordon?"

"I'm saying that I don't think that I have to do this job anymore. It's not making anyone happy, least of all, me. I don't see the point of wasting my life in this office anymore, infecting people with my negativity. You know, my negativity isn't special to me. Don't fool yourself for one second into thinking that I'm the only person who thinks that way. Don't fool yourself into thinking that all these people who work away at their desks aren't fighting off boredom every hour and dreaming about tropical vacations they may never take. A lot of people feel the way that I do; I'm just not that good at hiding it."

I got up and made my way for the door. He stared at me with big eyes.

"And by the way, it's Gordie. And in case you missed it, I quit."

I walked out and closed the door softly behind me. No need to make a scene and affect more negativity in the office. But I didn't feel negative at all. Not one little bit.

Gusto got.

Chapter 27—I'm Canadian

"You're a shit crazy bastard!"

"Yeah, yeah, I know."

"I can't believe that you did it, muchacho! I wish I was there, it sounds beautiful!"

Jose put his arm around me and laughed, a dreamy look in his eyes as he imagined me telling off my boss and walking away from my horrible job. All of them were there that night to celebrate, and although there were moments where I felt like it wasn't quite real, I felt pretty damn good about myself.

Business Dan, Stan the Man, Roger, Adventure Tim and Georgie were also on hand to celebrate. They all brought beer and tequila with them, good friends that they are, and Business Dan even broke out a box of real Cubans to cap the night off. The hermanas knocked themselves out cooking plate after plate of delicacies for us and joined us in the many tequila toasts, holding up every bit as well as their hermanos. Mama was there too, although she didn't look overly amused, and Papa, well, he was over the moon with joy.

"Hordie, you are a good boy. You've done a brave thing today, to walk away from a bad job in the hope of a better life. People are going to call you crazy and they will be right—but you will be one step closer to happiness than any of the normal bastards out there!"

"Hear, hear!"

"What was it that you said again? Come on, Gordo, tell us the story again! Repeat that famous last line!"

"Yeah!"

"Tell it again, Gordie!"

"The story! The line!"

"I said—and by the way it's Gordie. And in case you missed it, I quit."

"In case you missed it, I quit!"

"Yeah! That's telling the man!"

"That's it!"

"Let's have a toast!"

We put our tequila shot glasses together over our heads and then, in unison, we yelled;

"And in case you missed it, I quit!"

"Woo!"

We drank. It was the first of many. I knew that the worry was going to set in tomorrow and that I would have backlash to deal with, but for tonight, I was just about the happiest person on the planet. I felt free. I felt like I had just broken out of prison and that it had been easy. The prison that I had broken out of was the prison in my mind and now my mind was free again. I felt like anything was possible, like everything was possible. Like the world was mine and I could go anywhere I wanted, whenever I wanted. I hadn't felt like that since I was a naïve undergrad in university, partying it up in Montreal and going on 2am poutine runs and dreaming that life was still going to be a sweet ride . . .

We laughed, we drank, we ate, we sang songs, we attempted to dance, we smoked cigars. Margarita even made me a cake! It was a huge thing that almost fell over when they carried it into the apartment. It took two hermanos to carry it in. It was a fantastic night and it was even better because all of my little family was there. Not my family members, but the people that I felt at home with.

The members of my family met the news with a mixture of shock and indignation. Needless to say, they were a lot less impressed with my story. My father wanted to know why I thought I was better than this life, why I thought that I had the right to a 'fun' job when work was work and I had had a respectable position. My mother wanted to know what was the point of raising me and educating me to the best possible degree, only to have me 'throw it all away.' My brother just thought that I was crazy and my sister didn't say anything at all. My brother in law told me not to borrow money from them.

Despite my best efforts to block it all out, it did bring to mind all the doubts and fears that I knew that I would have. It was scary and uncertain to know that I was leaving a lifetime of job security and material comfort for . . . for something that had no shape or form, but plenty of promise. I had visions of myself on the street or delivering pizzas. Of course, that's what they wanted me to have. That's what they expected. I was the dumb dreamer of the family once again.

The next day, I went back to the office to clean it out a bit and meet with HR. I had given my two weeks' notice and it wasn't exactly a convenient time of year, but that didn't matter to me. It was never a convenient time of year to lose someone in the office, but that wasn't going to stop me anytime soon. I was sitting in my cubicle, cleaning out my inbox and trying to do up some briefing notes for the next guy who would get my job, when I came across those job ads from the NHL site. There were a few sales jobs in California. I would never, ever dream of joining the Ducks after the Cup Run ended in disaster. But there was San Jose and there were also the LA Kings . . .

Nobody answered when I called the Kings. It must have been lunchtime or something. I was thinking of getting back to work, but then I decided to give San Jose a quick one before heading off to lunch myself. Adventure Tim had promised me lunch at my favourite steakhouse and I was really looking forward to having a good juicy steak and cold beer. But I had time for one quick call.

"Hello, you've reached the San Jose Sharks sales department. Josh speaking."

"Hi Josh. My name's Gordie Howard and I'm interested in applying for a sales job with the Sharks."

"Do you have any previous sales experience?"

"I've worked retail in the past. Most of my recent experience has been within a government office, but I'm looking for a change."

"Did you see the job ad posted through the NHL website?"

"Yes, I did."

"So I'm presuming that you're somewhat competent when it comes to talking hockey?"

"Hey, man. I'm Canadian."

There was a moment of silence and then a soft chuckle on the other end of the line.

"Where are you from?"

"Ottawa."

"Ah. Sorry about the Senators."

"You're not the only one. But good on California. I guess it's the place to be soon enough for all the armchair hockey guys."

"Armchair hockey?"

"Yeah, you know, the fans who can't play worth a darn, who just watch from the sidelines, but direct the game as much as possible by shouting at the screen?"

"Are you one of those guys?

"You bet I am. I always think that I can change the course of the game for some reason. I coach from the sidelines, I yell out plays, I make calls, I give advice. I'm a fan."

"You definitely sound like one. Are you willing to relocate?"

"Willing and able."

"You wouldn't mind moving cross country to the States to talk on the phone every day to sell tickets to people who like the beach more than ice?"

"I'd throw everything in the car and drive over myself if given the chance. I love hockey and I want to find a job in something I love. The wisest man I know told me to make something of what I love, and that's what I'm trying to do. And if it means starting at the bottom, well, I guess I'll take it."

"Do you have any dependents? Wife, children, dog?"

"None of the above."

"How soon could you start?"

"Are you serious?"

"Yeah. How soon?"

"That's it? You're not even going to interview me or look over my CV?"

"We can get through those formalities later. Look, I'm the manager here in sales. You'll see my name on the website organization. I just picked up the phone because one of the staffers is on a cigarette break, filthy habit. You don't smoke, do you, Gordie?"

"No sir."

"Good. Because it's not healthy and it doesn't project the image that we want to have. Plus, all the breaks are bad for business. Listen, son, I've hired a lot of retail and business people in the past for this job and as good as they are at what they do, they can't talk hockey. They don't have a sense of the game or why it's special and that comes through to clients, whether it's on the phone or in person. They lack knowledge, but more than that, they lack passion. And you can teach any idiot the basics of the game, but you can't teach them to love it, so they don't sell it. I'm through hiring those types. I want more people like you, people who are dynamic, motivated and know what they're talking about. I need your enthusiasm to shine through and to get people buying up seats. Are you in?"

"I am so in!"

"Great. How soon can you start?"

"Give me two weeks, sir, I'll be in San Jose."

"Two weeks is great. I need you as soon as possible to get us started on selling next season's tickets. We're already behind schedule. Fall's coming around fast. I'm going to give you the fax number here so that you can send your CV to HR and they can start figuring things out. You're also going to need a work visa, but we'll figure that out once you get here. Any questions?"

"Can I get tickets to the game for me and my friends?"

He roared with laughter. I wasn't sure if that was a good thing until he came back on the line.

"You can have an entire row to yourself once the season begins! Goddamn, I could use 8 of you, Gordie! That kind of enthusiasm really gets people. Take this number down . . ."

It was all happening. It was actually happening. Trembling, I took the number down and got all the details put together. I was dazed while going through the paperwork and the last of the formalities. But it had actually happened. As simple as that.

When I went to bed that night, I still couldn't believe it. I kept replaying the conversation again and again in my mind and still it seemed like someone else's dream. But a couple of days later, the letter of offer for my job came through the fax machine with the NHL logo on it—more specifically, the San Jose Sharks one. I stared at it in disbelief. It was real. Then there was all the paperwork for my American work visa. This was not a dream. It was a dream come true.

Chapter 28—California Dreamin'

It's true what they say about when things are meant to happen. The universe really does conspire to make things happen in those times. The process to get my American work visa went smoothly and I managed to find a rental property online in San Jose. It was a studio apartment about a block away from the HP Centre, where most of the other staff members lived. It was sort of funny to be moving into a tiny place where the bed was in the wall, but hey, it was all part of the adventure and it was what I could now afford.

My family tried to be happy for me, even though it was clear that they thought that I was regressing to some sort of adolescent phase of my life. My mother clearly hoped that I would get over it, while my siblings were excited at the prospect of having an excuse to visit California in February. My brother was the only family member who seemed genuinely happy that I was headed for a career in sports. He said that I was living the dream for both of us, and maybe I was. There was a silver lining after all.

But while my parents had grim faces on the day that I left, they still wished me well. I was hopeful that they would understand in time. To show me that they were still my parents, they did what every well-intended parent does when their children act foolish; they gave me some money before I left.

"Just enough so that you don't fall behind."

"I know."

"I'm not going to pretend that I like this, Gordon. But you have to do what's best for you."

My mother frowned up at me. My father had the same look on his face, equally grave. I gave them both a hug. As I hugged my dad, I asked,

"You're coming to visit me at some point, right?"

"Make sure you have a place with a pool."

We laughed and I knew it was going to be alright. For the first time in my life, I felt too proud and hopeful to feel chastised. I knew in my heart that what I was doing was right and that would become obvious to everyone else one day. With one last wave to the family, I headed home to load up my car and get started on my big move.

Georgie kept the apartment for himself and Consuela, who was moving in as his fiancée, much to everyone's delight. Papa threw me a huge fiesta before I left, complete with champagne. Margarita made me food for my trip; it was a sweet gesture and she put her arms around me and told me that I should always be a dreaming fool rather than dreamless, dead soul.

Saying good bye to everyone was harder than I thought it would be. The guys were all excited for me and promised to visit once I got my game tickets. I had stacked my car with all my worldly possessions and was ready to make a long cross country drive to my new job with the NHL. I couldn't believe it.

There was almost nothing that I wanted to take with me. I had clothes, shoes, a few books, some music, my laptop, but pretty much nothing else. I would get new furniture in California. It was truly a clean start.

My service ended with the government. I got a good pension and benefits package, as well as a good payout of vacation that I never had the chance to take while putting in so much overtime. It added up to a good amount; enough to start my new life on. I knew that my pay wasn't going to be much in California, but that wasn't a big deal. I would have enough to make a decent living and I could work my way up in the organization. This was a career, not just a job that I was moving to.

I was also excited to be driving there. It had always been one of those romantic notions that I had, taking a road trip across America and seeing all its wonders and oddities. It felt like I was a roamer, one of those free spirits who took to the open road. I felt like an old soul come back to life.

Everything excited me. The thought of the trip, the thought of exploring a whole new city, living in a state where I could see the ocean, heading to the beach, working for the NHL. I was excited in a way that I hadn't been in a long time.

I had said what felt like a hundred farewells over the last few days, but I needed to talk to Papa most of all. He walked me to my car where I was ready for my long trip. The guys had gifted me with a Senators jersey so that I wouldn't forget about them and my team. It was Alfredsson's, of course.

Papa and I looked at each other. It was an emotional farewell, I could feel that, but it wasn't goodbye. Still, I felt like I had to say something special.

"I want to thank you, Papa. For saying what you did, but also, for believing in me. I know it's one thing to say all the right things, like telling people that you want them to be happy, but it's another when they're really behind you, like you've been. I really feel like you've been in my corner."

"You're not getting rid of Papa, you know. I will be driving myself down to California to see you one day and I expect you to have one of these ready and waiting for me."

He handed me a bottle of tequila and winked.

"I will be driving a minivan and bringing all the family with me. And I might have grandchildren with me."

He winked again. Georgie and Consuela. What a thought.

"You're all welcome, you know that. I'll try to find some room for you."

"You will have a big house one day where you will have to house us all when we come down to see some games. And you will have to show us around—I expect you to know all the good Mexican restaurants."

"It will never be what las hermanas can cook."

"True, true. You know that you will be missed by all of us. Especially me."

"I'll miss you a lot, too, Papa. I'll be sure to call when I need to hear a friendly voice."

"You will always have me to call. Always."

We hugged each other like a true father and son. I knew that he meant it. All of it.

I had to get going before it got too dark out. I wanted to put in some good hours on the road while the days were still long. I got behind the wheel and thought of all the things that I was looking forward to seeing along the way, all the sites, all the states that I would cross. I thought of the landscapes and landmarks that I would pass, the roadside diners where I would stop for burgers and coffee, the pictures that I would take to remind me of one of the greatest journeys of my life. And the long hours of solitude, where I would be left alone to dream of all that lay ahead for my future, which now looked like something bright, wonderful and unknowable.

I had a long road ahead of me.